DEUCE DEUCE TO Love

A Shot at a Second Chance

LAKISHA LOVE-PETTIS

CONTENTS

FOREWORD

Since LaKisha was a child she's always loved and enjoyed writing letters, poems and short stories. To see her finally print and produce a written book is amazing and reinforces the reality that she is a resilient person that finished what she started. It has been exciting to read excerpts from her book that created my desire to read it in its entirety as I've become immersed in the reading. Job well done!

Love is life, liberty, and loyalty. #4L

INTRODUCTION

There is no doubt that tragic life experiences can be traumatically impactful. The idea that one's past doesn't impress upon their reality is questionable. Throughout the journey of this book, you will read how a young girl witnessing her mother being physically abused impacted her, and how those moments became the catalyst for her immediate need to defend any sign of harm. She once experienced being grabbed by a guy in a nightclub because she ignored him and refused to date him, even though he said he adored her. She fled home from the club to get her "deuce deuce" and returned with the intent to shoot to kill!

Why? Because in her mind, she had already made the decision that she would never be like her abused mother. She determined that she would never allow a man to put his hands on her or allow anyone to control her life. It was this trauma and emotional triggers that came with it that would eventually turn her life into tragedy!

Resilience became her middle name as she found herself learning to navigate through dangerous territory and the many people and circumstances that had been unhealthy negative influences. Yet, consistency and resiliency became the strength that led to success. Victoria truly learned how to become victorious in spite of her dreadful circumstances.

This book is about the transformation of a traumatized girl who became a young lady, mother, professional career woman, and ultimately a wife despite the many turbulent situations that could have undoubtedly made her a statistic. Surrounded by weapons of destruction in various aspects of her life, she could have easily gone ballistic, but instead followed her heart, and hence the title of the book: Deuce Deuce to Love.

This compilation of stories is intended to provide encouragement, strength, confidence, and motivation to all those experiencing difficult times in their life. Each chapter tells the story of how Victoria dealt with numerous assaults on her life, and how she ultimately overcame them, and what she learned from them. Not only did these awful experiences make her a stronger person, but now she can help others who are facing similar challenges to learn from her mistakes. This book will be a valuable resource for anyone who is struggling with chaotic situations in their own life. It is a reminder that you are not alone, that more is possible, and that you can overcome any challenge if you are willing to fight for it.

CHAPTER 1

A Shot From The Hip - It's Her World...or So She Thought

Victoria was the name given to her by her parents. It would remind her of the pure elegance of her existence, and that she was the queen of their world. In the Fall of 1977, Victoria's reign began. She was a cutie no doubt... weighing 7 pounds and 6 ounces. Skin soft as butter, hair fine as silk, with a complexion that illuminated the very essence of beauty.

No doubt their little girl would light up everyone's world, as she was the first grandchild on both sides of the family. Victoria was born in the heart of the District of Columbia, at Columbia's Hospital for Women. As a second-generation native Washingtonian, everything about her would resonate with her being a DC girl! Yes, all that saw her, loved and adored her, and would become a part of her world even at a very young and tender age.

Her hair grew to become like long pressed silk sheets, with a brightness to her skin tones, so that by the age of two it was not unexpected that this young beauty would participate in pageants at many places, but mostly in her neighborhood recreation center which would be an important birthplace to many of Victoria's memories, whether good or bad. However, her life would become severely interrupted as her parents relocated to Northeast DC for a short period of time. It soon became evident that despite how beautiful one's baby is...no child can keep a couple together. No man or woman can make their partner stay and the life lesson became realized that sometimes you just have to let 'em walk away. This was a critical moment that would no doubt shape Victoria's life...as a result, she ultimately grew up without living with her mother or father.

From the age of 3 until she was about 9, Victoria became the princess. No longer living with her parents, she was like the real-life doll baby to her auntie and her friends. No one could tell her anything, but she could definitely tell you everything and expressed herself quite uncensored, so she was told. Yes, Victoria was Miss Sassy for sure, with hair now down her back and custom-made clothes galore. She was truly a mini fashionista with an attitude that matched. Her frowns also came along with her, making her the leader of the mean girl's club. Pretty and petite, she was made to believe that everything was always about her, and that it was her world, and she could have anything she wanted. She talked to anyone anyway she please and no one would say a thing. Little did she know that this false perception would be the anchor of her soul and made her become what one considered to have an ice-cold heart. Victoria not only had beauty and looks, but she was also super smart and all about her books. She was taught early on by the older ladies in her life that she needed to be equally intelligent as she was pretty.

As life continued, there were moments that would become so impactful to Victoria as a girl. On one occasion, Victoria was reunited with her mother who had now become a mom to other children. At this time in Victoria's life, she embraced the reality that she was a big sister with brothers. For years her older boy cousin had been her protector and brother. So, the idea of going to live with her mother meant pure bliss even though it would be in Southeast DC, a different part of town. However, that also meant that even though she was a young girl from uptown in her own world... the girls of southeast... lived in a different world. She would soon learn that being the new girl from uptown was an invitation to be in the "hated on" club. This meant that no one was willing to be her friend because she looked and dressed different. Yet, within days she became the leader of the girls' dance club and would also become the one to carry the school banner in the citywide annual DC school's parade. But not before some devastating blows would strike her life.

At this point Victoria had been at this school and living with her mom and brothers for less than 3 months. During this time, she experienced a culture shock of unfamiliar poverty. A week prior to the parade, as she and her younger brother were walking home, a group of "Linden Polin" girls surrounded Victoria and began pushing her back and forth. Well, little did they know, this pretty uptown girl had an uncle that was an amateur boxer that taught Victoria how to box. She learned to always protect her face with one fist in front of her face, and the other at her chin line. So, during this bullying moment, Victoria stated on more than one occasion that she didn't want to fight! But this had become a moment of truth. She knew it was either win or lose. She found enough inner strength to deal such a powerful blow that resulted in her opponent leaving with a bloody nose. This gave Victoria and her brother a pathway to continue walking home unbothered.

This experience was the beginning of revealing her resilient nature. Surprisingly, Victoria and her opponent would become friends later in that week and even formed a dance routine together. However, that newfound friendship would end sooner than expected on the day of the parade, which became Victoria's last day at that school and living with her brothers.

Upon arrival at the school to get on the charter bus, Victoria's mother was informed that Victoria needed tan pants, and her mother agreed to go across the street to buy them, but in that moment, things drastically took a turn for the worse. She watched in shock as her mother, who had no control of who she was, and neither did the man that she was with, have an episode that played out in front of the entire parade participants. It was incredibly embarrassing to watch, Victoria got to witness how drugs changes people's personality and causes them to have debilitating habits. The vice of drugs had proved to become such a disruptive force in her life. From that point on, Victoria's real hatred for drugs began.

A classmate that lived across the street provided a new pair of pants that unfortunately were too small for Victoria. Needless to say, the days of custom clothes being made by her grandmother were over, but instead, now they were bought from low end stores that matched the significant income difference. These moments would follow Victoria throughout the course of her life as a reminder of how she did not want to be. She returned back uptown and to her old neighborhood school with the assurance that family always comes through. To her benefit Victoria's mother agreed that moving back was in the best interest of her daughter. In spite of that traumatic situation, better days were ahead.

While the return to school uptown was like a breath of fresh air, it also meant a cluster of new challenges would surface. During the time Victoria was welcomed back by her childhood friends, there were three girls that couldn't stand her, but it never bothered her. In fact, she laughed at their behavior because she knew she was liked by most, and loved by all the teachers because she was super smart and always made the honor roll. Things immediately picked right back up to where they left off. Her grandmother resumed making her custom clothes, her aunt and cousin bought her expensive clothes and jewelry, and don't forget about the one boy that she knew since pre-kindergarten, was crushing on her! Life was good! Victoria thrived as her life bounced back to where it was before and now, even better! As a result, Victoria's confidence was strengthened so much that some even considered her to be vain.

That vanity coupled with her mean girl personality deeply annoyed the two specific girls that didn't like her, which happened to be a set of twins. On one occasion when she was leaving school while walking home, one girl followed her and approached her and said, "Oh, you think you pretty." and Victoria replied, "No I don't think I'm pretty...I know I'm beautiful!" The look on the bully's face was that of shock, rendering her speechless. This was a victorious moment for Victoria as she was able to walk into the house unscathed.

The most daunting moment was when Victoria was in the sixth grade and had been selected as the Ambassador of the Netherlands representative for her elementary school to go to the United Nations in New York City! This was a pivotal moment, as only a few students from Washington DC were selected. Yes, it seemed like Victoria was at the top of the world again. Well, that was until the tale of the two twins. On one particular day, the sixth graders were in science class. The twins were actually much older and belonged in the eighth grade but had stayed back to make up their grades. This made the twin students be in the same class with Victoria.

Well, in Victoria fashion, she felt that she was a hotshot that could say whatever she wanted without any consequences since she never received any... until the day she told one of the twins to be quiet during science class. Then, upon returning to their home room class, Victoria purposely let the swinging door close right in the face of one of the twins. But what came next was unimaginable!! Victoria had just walked into the classroom and had begun talking to her teacher, then her school crush who later became her boyfriend also entered the class with several other students. He had witnessed the disruption in science class that continued to be a disturbance in home room.

As Victoria walked to her desk, while singing in her custom-made red corduroy dress that had pockets in the front, one of the twins tapped her on the shoulder. Just as Victoria turned around to see who tapped her shoulder, one twin had her first balled up, cocked her arm back and shot from the hip so hard that she fell on the floor in between the school desks! In a royal manner, Victoria reacted quickly and caught herself before hitting the ground. She immediately walked out of the classroom without saying a word and headed for the bathroom.

This walk was one of shame, but she held her head high even though she felt like she was walking in a slow-motion twilight zone. She literally saw stars when she was hit. All of her classmates were stunned, and her boyfriend had a look of tremendous concern. However, Victoria knew she couldn't stop for anyone as her pride would not allow her to stop. She knew it was only a matter of moments before the tears started to flow... and they did as soon as she walked through the bathroom door. She had never been hit before and especially not in her beautiful face.

Fortunately, only the side of her eye was red but ultimately caused a bruised ego. However, it didn't take long for her resilient spirit to emerge. It was a moment of clarity for her to devise a vengeful plan for the twins to be removed from the school. Fortunately, the teacher, who witnessed this act of bullying, had already notified the principal. This would be the last of them as they both had a history of incidents getting them expelled and they were too old to remain in that school anyway. Ironically, it would be decades later before Victoria would see those twins that taught her the first lessons of navigating through some of the difficulties of life. It was a striking reunion because the twins looked exactly the same.

Lesson learned: Be careful about how you treat people. Revenge is never sweet.

CHAPTER 2

Bringing the Heat: Memoirs
of a Transitioning Teen

Summertime uptown Northwest DC, Brightwood area, meant block parties, and fun family events. Georgia Avenue Day was soon approaching. It was also the summer that intrigue, harsh realities, and decisiveness would become highlights of Victoria's life. It was roughly the summer of 1988, on a cool evening that came with a brisk breeze. Victoria's mother came to visit, accompanied by a male friend. The visit started out as nothing less than blissful. At this point in Victoria's life, she's still very much unaware that her mother was still very ill, battling her vices. However, on this particular night, Victoria's mother was getting worked up bringing on the heat and told Victoria she wished she was never born. Victoria felt a cold chill go up her spine. This was the moment that would define her for the rest of her life. It was in that moment that she had vowed to live up to that reality. Despite having studied the Bible and attending Christian meetings regularly, a wall had been instantly erected around Victoria's heart.

That night also left a constant reminder that her mother also told her that "she was cold-hearted". Other than her family and two close friends, Victoria could not seem to maintain any healthy relationships. She had become bitter, feeling unwanted, unloved, and broken-hearted. This experience became the motivation for her to bring the heat and become the best in whatever she did in her life, as long as it didn't involve having to care about other people's feelings. Also, in that moment, the era of her personal resiliency began. This was her time to develop a strategic plan to bite the bullet and endure the infliction by the words of her mother. This was difficult because she knew that although she was feeling broken, she needed to understand how to heal. She also knew that was not her mother but the vice that controlled her thoughts.

Over the next few years, Victoria became withdrawn from the love of her life although she thought it was only "puppy love". She went to the United Nations as a school representative and graduated middle school with honors. She participated in the youth at-risk program, which became a defining moment that would steer the next course of her life. In these years, she learned how tragedy would show up as people through the constant trauma she experienced. She also learned how detrimental the DC drug era was to the lives of people in the community including her peers that were in the program.

The program would convene rival DC neighborhood schools and put them in a conference room for hours where they all had an opportunity to become very vulnerable in sharing their life experiences. Of course, Victoria knew her life was severely impacted by the words of her mother and was unafraid to speak first. So, although she won an award for being the first to share, the stories of her peers that followed revealed situations of chronic child abuse, neglect, witnesses to murder, bullying and a life of crime. The stories were all so horrendous.

It was during that week-long session of being vulnerable that Victoria learned empathy and forgiveness. And during those rough moments of listening that she realized that the critical conversation with her mother was not the end of the world, but she also realized that she needed some additional healing and that the offer of a yearlong mentorship and counseling was just what she needed. In fact, it was during this time of newfound consideration of the feelings of others that Victoria's voice was heard.

The year was now 1993 and Victoria had started to learn how to lead by her voice and not just rely only on her looks. And, although she encountered deceptive friends that eventually became foes, she now wanted to focus on the purpose of doing good for others. She became involved in community engagement affairs that gave her the opportunity to interview the first black female Madam Mayor Pratt-Kelly of the District of Columbia. She attended a youth gala with well-known journalists and newscasters.

All the while, she revisited the idea of searching for the truth through her personal Bible studies. However, the end of 1994 took a turn for the worse that put Victoria in a very dark place, so much so, that she considered attempting suicide. Fortunately, in that moment, she called on a close friend, reached out to close family and relocated to Maryland. After intense counseling and reaffirmation from her family that she was safe and protected. It was at that moment of Victoria's life that she felt both defeated and victorious. It was also in that moment that Victoria's mom answered the call for help and to Victoria's surprise any words that her mother had spoken would no longer sting but rather calmed her, covered her, and healed those deep-rooted wounds.

Lessons learned – Be the voice of change. Learned behavior can be transformational and become the positive guiding force in life.

CHAPTER 3

Scared Straight - A DC
Girl Saved by Skyline

I t was senior year, after the Fall of 1994, when Victoria moved out of DC to a suburban area known as Skyline. This was a major setback for Victoria because she had to leave her friends. But she had also met a guy who had become her male best friend. While dating another guy, she vowed that she would never again deal with someone that lived a hustler's life. It was a few Skyline nights that Victoria first learned to fill the sky with "puffs" of herbal air. It initially seemed fun, but she always remembered that it was those type of vices that negatively impacted her life. She learned to pay attention so that she did not repeat the cycle.

During the months of living in Maryland, she was now living with her paternal grandmother who loved her from within but had an evil way of showing it. Although she hadn't seen her for years, she showed Victoria what it meant to be a family. The next nine months would turn out to be the best months of her life, just prior to the tragedy that would occur just after graduation.

During this time of living in Maryland, riding the school bus with others from the neighborhood, Victoria also gained friends. Although it was more males than females, real friendships were made with guys who became like family along with the ones that were actually related to her. Although Victoria appreciated being there, she felt stuck there on the weekends because unlike the city, the metro buses did not run on the weekends. Victoria would literally have to call her male friends to come get her any time she wanted to go out.

She got to live her life without any responsibilities, and she had the freedom to come and go as she pleased. She was only taking trigonometry and English in school because she had enough credits from her high school in DC. This afforded her the privilege of taking cosmetology and working in the guidance office. Working in guidance office was one thing that made Victoria feel like she was at home in DC. Her summers were often spent working in an office under the former DC Mayor Marion Barry Summer Youth program every year since she was 13 years old. She initially started working with her aunt at the Securities Exchange Commission a few days a week. No doubt, being the new girl in the guidance office made her become very popular, and almost immediately, she linked up with other ladies that were from DC now attending the same Maryland school. This resulted in her having friends that were genuine, and with boys that she could share a platonic relationship with as well.

Victoria was a world traveler and she missed traveling with her maternal family, who still remained supportive in every point in her life. They sponsored her trip when her paternal grandmother refused to cater to her or make her feel entitled. Victoria even tried working at a movie theater and at a sandwich shop because she was trying to be self-sufficient. No longer living in DC meant no random trips to the mall. Gifts of money and clothing were less frequent. Now it meant planning for what you want and earning those funds, which was a lesson that she didn't realize she needed. This was a hard lesson to learn and came in the moment when her grandmother called her the "B" word because Victoria refused to use products or eat food that were not brand names.

Interestingly enough, although Victoria lived with her paternal grandmother, she didn't live with her father. Unbeknownst to Victoria, her father also had vices, and in an effort to defend his mother's position, he slapped Victoria in the face in an effort to discipline her. In that moment, Victoria's immediate reaction was for her to defend herself and so she went in the kitchen and got a steak knife and threatened to call the police if her father ever put his hand on her. Victoria saw this as a tragic experience because he had never disciplined her, and she always saw herself as daddy's girl. Victoria's heart was broken, and instead of being scared straight, she fled by jumping out of her bedroom window at Skyline.

This led her to living back in the city of DC even though she hadn't graduated yet. She knew that it was time for her to leave. She vowed to never go back or to talk to her father. Just thinking about it only raised her need to defend and protect herself. This impacted her ability to respect and trust that men could protect her, as well as with other situations with males in her life.

Victoria went on to graduate high school with honors and although her maternal grandmother didn't attend, Victoria never forgot how she was there when she needed her and that meant she had to ensure the relationship was mended...years later.

Lesson Learned: Materialistic things are never more important than family. So, honor your family while they are here, because when they are gone, it will be too late.

CHAPTER 4

Riding Shotgun - Tragedy
and Trajectory

Graduation day had come and gone, and Victoria was back living in DC temporarily after several stints of living with friends. This time was spent living life on another level of fun, so she thought. This time consisted of drinking gin, being lavished with gifts of clothes, jewelry and cars from her guy, even though it always came at a price. She spent most of her time alone because he was in the streets, and there was no longer an adult in the home telling Victoria what to do. It seemed like it was the time of her life as she had always thought of herself as a good girl that studied the Bible.

But she did not realize that not taking advantage of an opportunity to attend Howard University was a privilege, especially since her legal guardian worked there and costs would've been minimal. Instead, she decided to get a job. In Victoria's eyes, it was as if she had navigated successfully to adulthood with a newfound life of love and fun. But like all things ungodly... the moments of pleasure and fun would soon come to an end.

The date was September 17, 1995. A day that will never be forgotten. A day that started out bright like the moment of sunrise. She woke up happy and looked forward to a day of going out and about. During this time, she didn't have to work at her job, which was at a clothing store. She took the job so that she could save her money to purchase her own car after obtaining her license. However, on this particular day, she was surprised with a gift of a car, that was a manual gear or stick shift, that didn't really matter because she figured that she had watched her guy enough that learning how to drive it would be easy. Well... under normal circumstances it would have been because she had practiced several times before obtaining her learner's permit, but never under any pressure.

One day when Victoria was out driving and shopping in Georgetown, she received a phone call to go to the local hospital. Who knew that day she would be going to the hospital three times. So, you're probably wondering...when did she get a "guy"...well her first love didn't work out because her mindset changed. Her focus had once again become all about her. When she met "her guy" in the mid 90's, whom she had been talking to during the summer before senior year, he was an only child that loved his mother. He treated his mom like a rose and from the friendly conversations that he and Victoria had, there was no other woman besides his mother that he loved and adored more. That day, they visited his mom, and as they walked out of the apartment the sun was so bright and in true rose fashion, she came to the door to see them off. While waving with the sun behind her, she asked Victoria the unimaginable question, "When will you all be giving me grandkids?"

Victoria laughed hysterically, for she already knew then that there was no way that she wanted nor had considered having children, yet alone at this sweet age of 17. In fact, no one could have ever thought that she was going to have one, because she was also considered a very vain and selfish person. Ironically, though many did think that she would have a child first because she was the first granddaughter, but to Victoria that meant nothing except that she deserved to be spoiled by everyone.

As they proceeded to leave the Silver Spring Maryland area just on the outer skirts of Washington DC along the 16th Street corridor, they decided to go shopping. They drove down the street and went through the park as they headed to Georgetown to hit the shops. The day was great with plenty of shopping and plenty of fun and laughter. They had an especially good dinner at one of her favorite restaurants right off Wisconsin Avenue. Just as the day started to settle down and the sun started to drop, was the moment they received that unforgettable phone call. Quite frankly Victoria just knew there could nothing be wrong with Rose as he always considered his mom to be invincible. But, as fate would have it, the call was from a local hospital, and the thought was to immediately just go.

However, on the way down to the hospital Victoria was told that they would need to switch cars. Unbeknownst to her, the car that was her gift was quickly taken away. Shortly after picking up a very small, yet petite car that was also a manual stick drive, they immediately left for the hospital. When her guy received the phone call, he was told that he needed to get to the hospital because his mother was sick. However, upon arrival, as they walked into the room would be nothing more than shocking. She lay there with her eyes open. Her guy kept asking, "Ma, you good? Ma, you good?" over and over. But there was no response. Victoria stood there in shock, realizing that his mom had already died.

It was all so surreal, because they had never thought it could happen…they had just said goodbye to her and did not know that it would be the last day they would hear her voice. At that moment Victoria started reflecting on earlier that morning, when his mother was asking her when her grandchild was going to be born. But if that wasn't enough, who would ever think that they would visit a hospital again within hours as her guy tried to grasp the reality of what was going on and the demise of his mother…there was no way that Victoria could prepare him for what was next.

About 7:00 PM, the phone rang again, and it was a call from his cousin's girlfriend. She was crying hysterically, so much so that Victoria could only hear every other word as she was trying to explain to him that she needed him to get down to Howard University Hospital ASAP. Not realizing what was going to happen next, all Victoria knew was that she needed to be there for her guy.

During this time, Hennessy became his best friend and there was nothing that she could do to convince him not to drive. Especially, since…and here's the surprise, she didn't even know how to drive a manual yet! He had vowed to teach her, but now she just needed to trust him…and she did. She thought to herself that she had not just watched him and so many other drivers that were experienced but that she would have learned herself. Now she would just have to trust him.

The events of the day were more than he could bare, knowing his cousin was fighting for his life because this was his favorite cousin, and the one that was like a real brother whom he loved so much. This was the cousin that introduced him to his lifestyle, and he was the one that always helped everyone. He had an infectious laugh… He was a family man that always had her guy's back, and Victoria's by extension. He was also an only child that was raised right and taught to be the one that had his family's back.

Thinking back, Victoria thought about times during the past summer when her guy's family would drive to North Carolina and his cousin would be there enjoying family, food and fun. They had a great time they had throughout the year, including summer nights spent at their aunt's house, where southern hospitality was always on the menu. That and a glass of gin always made a city girl smile.…Then during the new year celebration, everyone would go out in the fields and let off a shot at midnight…including Victoria. It was in the country that Victoria first learned how to shoot a "deuce deuce" gun.

They drove in silence to the hospital. All of those thoughts were running through Victoria's head, as she didn't want to believe the possibility that big Cuz could be dead. Upon arrival, it was as if they were walking on pins and needles. No one knew where to go, but by this time, her guy's cousin was out of surgery and in a room. The girlfriend was not able to call, due to her being in a state of shock. Victoria entered room 1238 with her guy. She could immediately see the sigh of relief on everyone's face to see big Cuz up, breathing on his own and talking slightly.

Apparently, there was an altercation that occurred in Northeast DC, and he was shot in the back with a shotgun that had an exploding bullet, after walking off. Victoria told him how glad she was that he survived. Her guy, now sitting at the bedside within his cousin's hospital room, started crying and told him about his mom, also about the only sister of his cousin's mom, who had died of cancer. As the hours passed, the streets had already started talking and as people poured into the hospital. There was one old head who told my guy what the streets were saying. By this time, it's well after 11:00 pm.

We had been in the waiting room for hours and apparently this shooting took place midday, which now meant the street walkers are out on the street. Shortly after leaving the hospital, they began heading to their home uptown, or so Victoria thought. They went south on Florida Avenue and headed to where Cuz's shooting took place. After turning on the block, her guy got out of the car. At this point, Victoria's anxiety rose as her guy approached the neighborhood junkie known as Stevie. So, Victoria knew at this time that she had to take control of the situation, so she climbed into the driver seat, just before another friend named D, came and got into the rear passenger seat. Shortly thereafter, as Victoria was adjusting her mirrors, she noticed that her guy had punched Stevie in the face! He punched him so hard that Stevie, who was well over three hundred (300) pounds, dropped to the ground, and laid there for almost 5 minutes, which was when they left.

In that moment, Victoria started panicking and she became afraid of what might happen next. As her guy approached the vehicle Victoria went back and forth with him about who was going to drive the vehicle. She expressed to him that she was afraid and that she did not want him to drive, because he was drunk and had been drinking and was full of rage, although it was rightly justified. She went on to tell him that although she did not know how to drive a manual transmission vehicle officially known as a stick shift, that she just wanted to make sure that she was safe.

However, her guy was adamant about not letting her drive stating that he had it and was able to drive the vehicle. So after about another 15 minutes of going back and forth Victoria felt defeated, losing the argument, so she rode shotgun. She immediately put on her seat belt because her guy was in a rage of fury and hit the gas pedal so hard that it sprinted through oncoming traffic on Florida Avenue. The car, being a small Toyota Chisel, was so small that it literally fitted on the sidewalk adjacent to Gallaudet University.

Victoria became so afraid because all she could think about was that things were not turning out as she planned. Although in the moment one would think that his actions were justified since he had just lost his mother, and he had just seen his cousin who was fighting for his life and who possibly could face paralysis. Victoria recognized in that moment that she wanted to choose life over death. As they veered onto the curve approaching 6th and Florida Avenue, she became even more terrified and started telling her guy that she needed to get out of the vehicle. He was not listening. It was as if he was in a zone and the only thing that he knew was pushing his feet on the gas pedal. So as the car proceeded on in a rage of speed, they approached North Capitol Street and Florida Avenue, which was a very busy intersection, she knew that she needed to jump out of the vehicle.

Victoria kept asking him to please let her out because she knew that her life was in danger.

At this moment all she could recall was her days growing up and her being told the scriptures from first Corinthians 15:33: "Do not be misled, bad associations spoils useful habits". Her life flashed in front of her. She began to rethink her life and all the ministries and Kingdom messages that were preached, came to the forefront of her mind. If only she had just listened, she would not be in this situation. However, none of that mattered to her guy. Just then, he made a right turn onto North Capitol Street and drove upwards towards their street, and as they were going under the underpass, it began to rain. Victoria was not prepared for what was about to happen next. As they passed through the underpass, the car flipped over as it hit the curb on the passenger side of the vehicle.

All the while, Victoria kept taking her seat belt off and putting it back on because she was waiting for that moment when she could just jump out of the vehicle, but that never happened. Victoria was knocked unconscious as the vehicle flipped more than 2 times, and on that last flip the vehicle was airborne. Victoria did not awaken until her guy had climbed out of the driver side of the vehicle and proceeded to pull the vehicle down which then jarred Victoria to consciousness. In this moment, it was a miracle that Victoria was still alive.

However, based upon the circumstances of that day, she knew that her guy was still heavily intoxicated and that the last thing he needed was to be arrested, having been an ex-felon with a previous juvenile record. Victoria immediately told her guy that once the ambulance arrived after they had placed the call. he needed to leave. There was no other option. At the age of 17, she wouldn't get in as much trouble. Although she put herself in jeopardy, all she knew at the time was to be supportive and to help someone who needed it the most.

Lesson learned: Reactions based on emotions can be reckless. Grief is real so take time to heal.

CHAPTER 5

Jumping the Gun - Diagnosis vs Beliefs

Returning to the aftermath of the car accident, Victoria was going in and out of consciousness in the ambulance, yet in her true vanity fashion, she told the medics do not cut up her clothes! However, that was the only time she spoke before arriving at Washington Hospital Center located on Michigan Avenue, which was less than a mile from the incident. Victoria didn't recall anything initially except the fact that lights were shining bright on her, and the room was full of doctors.

By this time, her family had arrived at the hospital as she had managed to tell her guy before they departed to call her grandparents. Upon arrival, although she was not baptized, Victoria knew some beliefs that she could never go against and that was on the matter of having a blood transfusion. Coincidentally, her stand on blood was already noted in her records when she had been going to that hospital for gynecological services. So, as Victoria laid there in bed, weighing 110 pounds, with a breathing tube down her throat, the doctors began telling her grandmother that a blood transfusion needed to be performed, because the amount of internal bleeding sustained was critical.

Victoria was in critical condition due to a lacerated liver, a collapsed lung, a broken pelvic and tailbone, two broken fingers on her left hand, a broken left knee, lacerated lip and tongue and here is the worst news of all…Victoria was pregnant and bleeding from the miscarriage! Who would've ever thought that the doctors would jump the gun and say that Victoria would only have four months to live! And that was the mighty blow.

In this moment Victoria felt like she had been shot, not once, but twice. Deuce deuce for sure as she not only was battling for her life, but now the loss of her unborn baby…and she never even knew she was pregnant. The doctors stated the unlikely probability of her survival, not to mention the fact that Victoria would never be able to have kids. Who knew that this new reality would be so painful to Victoria. This pivotal moment would resurface again in the years to come….

Now, at this point, Victoria was no longer living with her maternal grandmother and was now living on her own. She needed to reconnect with her mother and father due to her condition. It had been years since Victoria ever needed them for anything. Ironically during this time, Victoria's mother was three days clean and staying at Mt. Carmel Treatment Center, when she was contacted. Her father was also staying in DC but living in Southwest. It took some time to locate him…and time was of the essence. The first twenty-four hours after the accident were the most critical. There was literally no time to waste on a decision that needed to be made.

Victoria was placed on morphine due to the severity of her pain. As the morning sun rose, her parents appeared in her hospital room. They were so loving and for the first time in a long time, Victoria felt that they both loved their princess, which was the reason they named her Victoria. As her parents whispered her name softly to awaken her, Victoria opened her eyes and with tears of both joy and pain, she realized how much she needed them. In that moment, she just wanted to be held, just as they stroked her hair and embraced her gently, as she was badly bruised and breathing with the machine.

She managed to stay awake to listen to the doctors advising her parents of her diagnosis. The surgeon proceeded to inform Victoria and her parents that with the amount of blood that had been lost, a blood transfusion was necessary. Then they said that they would need to make an immediate decision, as they were currently draining the fluid within her chest, that was crimson red at the sight. They both looked at their daughter with eyes of fear and concern, as they were faced with the most daunting decision!

So, they both looked at Victoria and asked her what she wanted to do…meaning did she want to get the blood transfusion, even though they knew where she stood from a religious standpoint since they were not. The other option was to sign the Hospital Waiver Form which would relinquish Washington Hospital Center and all attending physicians from being held accountable for Victoria's demise, if she were to succumb to her injuries, by refusing to allow them to perform surgery or a blood transfusion. Before she was able to answer, Victoria's mother, who burst into tears and left the room, as she became very hysterical. In addition, the sudden impact of reality was hitting her, as here she finally was putting herself in a position to be there for and bond with her daughter. In one critical moment…a decision needed to be made that wasn't guaranteed either way to save her daughter's life and could still mean that she could lose her. Victoria, continued to listen and prayed, and in an instant, she received affirmation that was unexplainable. However, she knew that the best decision was to rely on her faith and honor her God just as she had done all through her life, although she had been struggling to fully align her lifestyle with biblical principles.

Victoria then proceeded to ask that her mother return to her side, but without any tears, for she knew that she would be healed. And just like that, the decision was final…Victoria would not be getting a transfusion. In fact, the doctors stated that she would have a low survival rate and they reiterated the fact that with the severe laceration of her liver and other injuries, she may only have four months to live. Over the next few hours, various doctors continued coming in the hospital room in an attempt to change her mind, but then the form to refuse a transfusion was signed.

Everything appeared so bleak, but little did they know that Victoria was on the road to recovery. No one would have ever thought that one's faith and inner mental ability to believe in something greater than themselves, or the doctors, would be so rewarding. Yet, rewarding was an understatement as Victoria's recovery was considered to be a miracle…literally. With the doctors feeling defeated, there was nothing more that could be done for Victoria.

Without performing surgery, she continued to lay in the hospital in a single position with medications being given gradually. However, after such a traumatic ordeal, no one could have imagined how Victoria's spirit and unwillingness to die literally kept her alive. By the fifth day in the hospital, Victoria's tube was removed from her throat, and she had begun breathing on her own, as the percentage levels of the fluid within her lungs had drastically been reduced. By the seventh day, Victoria no longer wanted to just lay in the bed and asked if they could help her walk around her room and in the hallway with crutches although her knee was broken and in a cast. By the eighth day, Victoria had begun to make arrangements to find somewhere to live with a family member that would help take care of, but not baby her.

Victoria knew that there was only one person amongst her family that loved her dearly but would make her do things for herself in a firm but loving manner…and that was her aunt Emory. The more that Victoria thought about the moments growing up and her interactions with her aunt, the more confirmation she received that Aunt Emory was indeed the right person for the job. On one occasion that Victoria recalled, she and Aunt Emory weren't seeing things on the same page. Although Victoria felt being the first-born granddaughter gave her inalienable rights to entitlement, her aunt thought otherwise.

In fact, one day her aunt came to visit Victoria's grandmother, which was her aunt's mother, and demanded Victoria do some chores that weren't included in her weekly list. So, Victoria told her aunt, "No. I will not be doing those things, because it's not my week and you can't make me do anything, because you don't live here." One time when Victoria's grandmother wasn't home, this was finally her aunt's chance to discipline her niece, whom, by the way, had never received any harsh discipline, but always had a very smart mouth. Just as her aunt thought she was going to impart some physical discipline on Victoria…she had already made a call to her grandmother, while holding her Orioles memorabilia miniature baseball bat in her other hand. Upon realizing what was happening, her

Aunt Emory began yelling in the background about how disrespectful Victoria was being, and she deserved a beating.

At this point, Victoria laughed and then proceeded to say, "I wish you would hit me!" So, immediately, the grandmother told her daughter that she needed to leave her alone and that she needed to leave her house and come back once she got off from work. Well, no doubt, Aunt Emory was upset and proceeded to see how Victoria was being given so much consideration over her, especially since she was just her granddaughter. So, needless to say, Victoria stayed on the phone with her grandmother the entire time, until she walked in the front door and immediately began scolding her aunt Emory. Before you knew it, her aunt was out the front door. On the porch, Victoria stood behind her grandmother in the doorway, and started taunting her aunt and flinging her very long and pretty hair from side to side. This gesturing was meant to convey to her aunt that she was in charge and how dare she think that she would ever lay a hand on this pretty girl. At that point, Emory reached through the door and attempted to grab Victoria's hair and she had now become so upset that she called her niece a "vain heffa"!

As Victoria reflected on those memories, she also became empowered, because in hindsight, her aunt Emory was very intelligent and strong willed, but a gentle person that was loved by everyone. She had a personality of radiance and a laugh of thunder that was infectious. Yes, her aunt was the only one that she wanted to see at the hospital and the only one that truly loved her with a "no tolerance" grace. Finally, with Victoria's decision being made, on the ninth day after her near fatal car accident ordeal, she was released from the hospital and vowed to give life a second chance, despite the fact that her road to recovery would come with many obstacles, this would indeed be her second shot at life.

LESSONS LEARNED:
Doctors are practitioners that practice medicine. Faith is the assured expectations of things hoped for, so in this case belief prevailed over practice.

CHAPTER 6

A Real Pistol - The Hard
Road to Recovery

This September would be the month that Victoria turned 18, and she had begun to think about her life. She reflected on all that she had missed out on and the opportunities that had laid before her that she turned away because she wanted something more in the streets. While living with her aunt for almost six months, Victoria built resilience. The first two months were hard because Victoria had to lie on a wooden board. This was necessary because she could not turn left or right because of the injuries sustained to her liver. She was limited to the meals that she could eat and she could only drink water. The first sixty days were a blur primarily because she needed medications that included morphine, then oxycodone, and then eventually she only needed ibuprofen.

After four months, she became determined to no longer rely on her aunt giving her baths, but she knew that she needed to do it herself. One day Victoria asked her aunt just to run her bath water and to place her on a chair in the bathroom. Victoria knew that she needed to figure out how to get from the chair to the tub all by herself. On a few occasions, she even fell to the floor. Determined not to give up, Victoria believed that she was going to be able to bathe herself. She knew that it was a lot of work, but after weeks of trying she succeeded. She continued working on her breathing machine, inhaling, and exhaling to get onto the marker points, although breathing without coughing was a challenge. However, without a doubt, Victoria knew that failing was not an option.

By the summer of 1996, Victoria had miraculously recovered. During this time of recovery, Victoria's former guy had succumbed to drugs and alcohol. No one in her family wanted to see him and she herself wanted to focus on her recovery without taking on anyone else 's problems. By the time Victoria was ready to move on with her life she had asked her grandmother to help her to find her own place and she did. Victoria got an apartment in Northeast DC. Back then apartments were only $425.00 a month. One of her other aunts helped her to obtain employment and she worked two jobs so that she could sustain her lifestyle. At this time Victoria had officially obtained her license to drive and saved up her money to purchase her first vehicle which was a 1988 Mercury Zephyr Green Station Wagon. It was the cheapest car on the lot, but she felt proud because she purchased it with her own money that she earned all by herself. In fact, that year she also enrolled into a computer networking bachelors' program with Strayer University. In addition, she started back attending Christian meetings for a while as well.

The summer experience became a reality for Victoria again, and now she was old enough to go to an actual club and attend a DC GoGo party. This was an experience that in the past she had only attended at Georgia Avenue Day or when there was a special event at Nativity where she was able to see bands such as Rare Essence and the Backyard Band. This was an opportunity for her to experience the iconic clubs throughout the city, including the Metro Club and The Sugar Palace on Riggs Road.

During this time of recovery, Victoria is beginning to feel like a real pistol! She had received a second chance in life and a second shot to get it right. She decided that she was going to experience life to the fullest, and on her own terms, with experience being her greatest teacher. Victoria had come to realize that freedom also meant taking responsibility to maintain for herself. She had this newfound freedom over her life. However, freedom didn't come without a price. She was enjoying her new place and learning how to let go of the things that did not serve her. Her guy, having lost so much of himself after his mother's death and cousins near death experience, couldn't accept that she moved on without him. This was intensified by the fact that eventually his cousin died a few months later.

While Victoria was living uptown, she received a phone call from her ex-guy asking her to meet him. She agreed and met him at the "Yums" carry out on Georgia Avenue. He attempted to give her a leather coat and diamond ring that he got "hot" for her. She told him to keep it, and that she didn't want to be with him anymore. As she proceeded to get in her station wagon, he jumped on the hood of her car and threatened to stomp out the windshield if she drove off without giving him another shot. Well, this was a side to him that she never had seen with him, but when she recalled how he knocked out that guy in Northeast, she knew that she didn't want to ever be in the path of his anger. He was relentless and no matter how many times she attempted to tell him that they were over and that her family would never even approve, he couldn't accept the rejection.

Finally, she gave up and proceeded to start the engine of her vehicle and suddenly it was like pistol shots were fired as he completely shattered the windshield with his double sole Timberlands. At this point, Victoria became filled with so many emotions including rage, revenge and frustration. She jumped out of the driver side of the vehicle, facing northbound on Georgia Avenue, between Ingraham and Hamilton Streets Northwest. Then, she went into the trunk and got her crowbar out just as he jumped down. When he saw her with that crowbar and she was visibly upset, he began running. Having been a former track runner, she began chasing him. But once she realized that there was enough distance between the two of them, she threw the crowbar at his feet and ran to her vehicle and drove off.

She pulled around the corner enough so that she was out of his sight. She now needed to call her grandmother yet again, but this time asking if she could use the AAA membership to have her car towed to her apartment. Her grandmother understood the pain of her granddaughter's ex-guy, as she knew how it felt to lose a parent. Nonetheless, Victoria didn't want anything to do with him after the accident and the reality that she had lost her unborn child. She didn't want to be reminded of it all, and if she went back with him, she knew she could never move forward with her life. At least that was her thoughts then, and never anticipated who she would meet next.

LESSONS LEARNED: Resilience
is forward facing leaving the past without
looking in the rear-view mirror.

CHAPTER 7

Going Ballistic! The Psychopath!

It was the summer of 1997 and roughly two years after Victoria's accident, when she experienced her worse nightmare that nearly cost her her life. Up to this point, she had remained focused on herself without anyone else in her life. She was enjoying balancing work and her party life after months of recovery and receiving an eighty-thousand-dollar lawsuit from the car insurance for pain and suffering.

Victoria went to visit her grandmother and left her some money and a card and thanked her for all that she had done for her and her siblings. She then purchased herself a brand-new Mazda that she paid in full for ninety-five hundred dollars and gave her aunt anything she wanted for helping to nurse her back to health. Then she bought some Nike stock, as her grandfather had taught her the importance of investing, and of course she went shopping with her mom.

After having her vehicle for a month, Victoria needed to go to the District Department of Motor Vehicles, located on C Street Northwest. She had considered getting personalized tags, but then she thought about how vain that would be. Victoria often thought about the perception of things, her reality had become a dismal one, less than two years ago from the car accident that resulted in her also having a miscarriage. Although Victoria bought another car, she still kept her station wagon parked outside of her apartment that she had always hoped to get repaired one day. Victoria started catching the metro bus to work and the subway train. She would have post-traumatic stress disorder or PTSD from the car accident which included a fear of letting others drive or driving at night in the rain, and just felt safer taking public transit during the day.

Well getting back to the day at the DMV, after obtaining her license plates, as she walked outside, there was this nicely dressed guy with white linen pants, white shirt with the buttons opened showing his bare chest, with red suede Versace shoes. No doubt she was very impressed. He was clean-cut and freshly shaven. However, when he approached her and said she was cute, she politely thanked him for complimenting her but said that she was not interested. Well, he was persistent and then proceeded to ask her if she just had a few minutes for conversation. She agreed and found herself intrigued by his intelligence and his offer to take her on just one date before making a decision to take him up on his offer. He asked her for her number. She thought about giving him a fake number that she had been practicing in her head, but, once she started giving him the number, the correct one came out!

All she could do was smile, but wanted to kick herself as she walked away, because she had determined that dealing with a guy was a distraction from her goals right now. And just then, that guy, who will be referred to as Mr. Smooth, called the number and Victoria answered her cell phone. And in his raspy smooth voice, he says… "Yeah this is Smooth, and I was just making sure you didn't give me a fake number." She laughed and then turned around to see him standing where she had left him. She immediately thought to herself…Lawd I've met a psychopath.

Well, with that fleeting thought, she returned to her vehicle and thought about his conversation, and how that crazy moment now had started to look like an attractive offer. So, within the next two weeks, Victoria agreed to take Mr. Smooth up on his offer and go to dinner and a movie with him. She was impressed by his chivalry and upon taking her back to her car, since they agreed to meet at a mutual and public place. She had considered a second date. Within a few months, things started to move really fast – so fast that he asked Victoria to marry him! Yes, on this particular day, after going out on a date at the Washington, DC National Zoo, he proposed with a 2-carat diamond pear shaped ring. Victoria was blown away at how soon he had proposed and when she didn't give him a response, they left the zoo and headed to Northeast. In an effort to convince her to say "yes", he stopped by his godmother's house, which was the next best thing to his mother, who was deceased. This was significant, because the more that they got to know each other, the more it became apparent that Mr. Smooth was more of a street dude than what he first put on to be.

He had his own business and was an independent contractor that had been hauling dump trucks for years. He was single with no kids, and he had two sisters and two brothers. He was born and raised in Southeast Washington DC and Victoria knew that in itself was different from dealing with a guy from Uptown DC. But none of that mattered because he treated her like a queen. Although he hadn't traveled much, like Victoria who had gone on various family vacations growing up, including going to the country in the summer and Florida in the winter. The good news was that he was willing to travel outside of his comfort zone. In fact, he had never even been to Kings Dominion, which was in Virginia, and the best amusement park on the east coast.

It is important to note here that there was an age difference between them of about ten years, which was a new experience for her. And this seemed appropriate since this was her first adult experience as an 18-year-old, and with her own place and employment, she really felt grown. Although they were only dating, Victoria continued enjoying her work and life balance that now included traveling with a friend. When she went to the club at least 3-4 times a week, it was primarily by herself, until she met a few ladies that loved partying more than she did.

Mr. Smooth was very well known in the city and respected by most of the Southeast and feared by others that knew him in the city. Within the first four months, things became official, and Victoria was in a relationship with him and had accepted his ring, but only as a promise because becoming married was nothing that she had ever considered. In fact, since she was now still enjoying life the thought of marriage was far removed from her mind, even though many in her family appeared to be happily married for decades.

In addition, she was now only a couple months short of being 20, and her hair was the most important thing on her mind, so Victoria cut her very long and free flowing hair to a short and sassy style, cutting off almost 8 inches of hair, and dyed it red hot. She remained 122 pounds with an hour-glass shape and loved to wear designer clothes like Versace, Prada, Donna Karen and of course the classics by Ralph Lauren. She wore Guess or Calvin Klein slim fit jeans, when she dressed down with a sexy top to show off her curves. Because she was definitely a "dime piece" with looks and brains, Mr. Smooth knew that he had to always step his game up.

Soon, Mr. Smooth started staying at Victoria's place more often, because she didn't like going to his place, her neighbors started paying attention to the new guy in their hood. They themselves had already accepted her and they even flirted with her a few times, but she politely declined. But that never stopped them from watching her or approaching her. One day when she returned home from work, a young gentleman approached her dressed in a white t-shirt, blue True Religion jeans and a pair of fresh Jordan's, which were the only tennis shoes she wore besides high-top Reebok princesses when she would wear them.

Needless to say, she loved fashion and recognized expensive taste. She noticed that he also had on a Movado watch with diamond embedded trim. So, when he asked, very politely, if he could speak to her for a moment, while addressing her as Miss Lady, she acknowledged him and listened. He began to ask her, "so your boyfriend is Smooth from around 1000?" She then looked puzzled, because she had no clue as to what he was talking about. So, she then asked him, "I'm sorry, but who are you talking about?" The young gentleman proceeded to say, "ask your man…he knows what it is…" and then he walked off.

Well, this left Victoria feeling confused and pissed, because she knew that Mr. Smooth had been in the streets when he was younger but had told her that he was no longer a part of that lifestyle. But she continued to feel uneasy and curious, because she wondered what else she didn't know about him, that apparently everybody else knew? She felt compelled to ask him, but he wouldn't be home until later that night, since he was driving back from Richmond, Virginia with his job that had been away for three days.

So, the next day, when she got home from work, the same young gentleman approached her again, but this time, he waved to check to see if she had asked her "man" as he referred to him about being from 1000. She then told him no, but I'll see him today and ask him, as she quickly walked off feeling very uncomfortable and even a little bit afraid. Once she got into her apartment, which was facing the front on the corner of 21st Street and Maryland Avenue NW, she felt at home and comfortable. Mr. Smooth had brought her new furniture for both the living room and dining room. So, looking at her new things, she smiled and started preparing dinner as she was expecting to see him later that evening. Now back in those days, you had to go to the store to get a movie to watch on a VHS, which was a video home system that recorded movies using analog to watch at home. So, after she had prepared dinner, which consisted of steak, rice and broccoli… she left out to go to the Blockbuster. And yes, Victoria was a great cook as she was taught by the ladies of her family.

The summer nights in Northeast DC in her neighborhood, were very different from where she grew up in Uptown northwest. It was an adjustment, especially since she had grown up in a house all her life, so living in an apartment and seeing people and kids hanging outside was something she had rarely seen growing up. In fact, the only place children played when she was young was either the neighborhood recreation center located up the street from her home or in the backyard or the field in the alley behind her house. Nevertheless, on this late August evening, it was enjoyable to see everyone outside.

Now although Victoria was young in age, she had an old soul. She loved watching old movies and "oldie but goodie" songs, which was another reason that she enjoyed dating Mr. Smooth, because they often went to concerts to see groups such as the O'Jays and the Whispers. So, it was no surprise that she headed to the Blockbuster, to get her favorite movie called "Cooley High", which was a 1975 movie about some teen friends hanging out with people who really didn't have their back but was funny and heartwarming at the same time.

When she arrived back home, she noticed that there was not one person outside of her apartment anymore. In fact, there wasn't anyone in sight within a two to three block radius, either north or southbound. But Victoria didn't think anything else of it and she opened the door of the apartment building and went inside. Now once in the building, she realized that she never checked the mailbox, located in the hallway, so before going up one flight of stairs to her apartment unit, she retrieved her mail. When she got to the front door of her apartment, she looked outside through the window of the apartment building and still didn't see anybody, not any children, adults or pets were out. Nonetheless, Victoria went inside unbothered and proceeded to prepare the dinner table, that she kept well decorated. She had a glass dining table with gold and black chinaware, with her silverware rolled up in black fabric napkins, that she had learned how to prepare from her job at the senior living community center. In addition, she always kept a candle lit at the table to enhance the ambiance. When everything was prepared for dinner, Victoria grabbed a glass and poured herself her favorite wine, which was Alize, and the book that she was reading at the time, as she loved reading books often. Ironically, the book was called, "How Stella Got Her Groove Back", and it was definitely a great read.

She was ready to relax and enjoy the evening…when she hears BANG, BANG!! Glass broke as two bullets came flying one after another into her apartment from outside. The first bullet barely missed Victoria's head as she leaned up to get her drink, just as that bullet came inside and went into the wall where she laid her head on the couch, moments before. The second bullet came launching through the window and went straight through the wall and into the neighbor's house, where a sixty-two-year-old grandmother was grazed by the bullet!

This was an unimaginably terrifying situation that she was now placed in, and she had no clue as to why anyone would want to shoot at or attempt to kill her. She immediately started thinking and realized that her ex-boyfriend never knew where she lived and how she was able to get away from him. Now she was scared and begun having panic attacks as she was afraid to even stand up, for fear that someone would still attempt to shoot her. Frantic and alone, she crawled from the living room to the bedroom, fortunately the apartment had brand new fresh wall to wall carpet and high windows. Once she got to her bedroom which was on the side of the building, the blinds already pulled down with the curtains closed, she felt secure because no one could see her anymore.

She called Mr. Smooth on the phone, and he said he was on his way, off the 295 exit at Benning Road. All that Victoria could muster to tell him was that bullets came through the window. She still hadn't had the chance to tell him what the young guy had stepped to her about for the last two days, because in her mind, she needed to see him in person so that she could read his body language and look him in the eyes to make sure he would tell her the truth.

Within 20 minutes he was at her door and so were the Metropolitan "boys in blue" Police Department. Since there was no one outside, there were no witnesses and basically there was never a case. Victoria was so afraid to stay in the house, but even more afraid to leave. This was her home that no longer felt safe. Unbeknownst to her, when Mr. Smooth was in the house, he didn't have anything with him, but upon the police departure, he went back outside to his truck and had brought in a duffle bag. After a while they sat down at the table and started to eat while discussing the day's situation and the events leading up to that day. She also made inquiries regarding what she was told by the neighborhood guy.

At that time, he began to explain the details of his past in depth and how he went to prison for going ballistic and retaliating the murder of his brother. He shared that his mother died while he was incarcerated, and he wasn't allowed to attend the funeral. When Victoria asked how she died, he told her that it was from an overdose on drugs. In that moment, he became vulnerable, and tears followed from his eyes. She then had begun to share her experiences of when she witnessed someone in her family shooting dope with a needle in their arm and how she ran away for weeks after seeing that, and that she certainly could understand his pain. In that moment they bonded and initiated their first intimate entanglement. Now, as the morning sun rose the next day, reality had also set in.

Lessons Learned: Take time to truly get to know the person behind the smoky mirror as what looks good to you isn't always good for you. Protect your peace by knowing the red flags when they appear and leave as soon as you can.

CHAPTER 8

A Real Pistol!

Victoria expressed to Mr. Smooth that she no longer felt comfortable living in that neighborhood. So, as he gets out of the bed, he reaches for the duffle bag that lay on the floor next to him and proceeds to tell her that he will find them a place to live as he had previously been inquiring about buying a condo. More importantly, he told her she now needed to carry protection. Just as he said that she turned towards him, and he had already bought her a 22-caliber gun also known as a "deuce duece"! Back in those days, it was easy to purchase and register a gun for someone legally, especially in Virginia. As it turns out, the reason he was late getting to her house was because he had already started recognizing some of the neighborhood guys paying too much attention to him. He thought he was at a point in his life, that he could get away from living as the Psychopath that he was already known as by many. In fact, he was considered to be a notorious drug dealer and killer, but he had never told Victoria because he knew that she was a good girl that would certainly leave him.

He knew from the moment he spent the first date with her, that she was different. Now Victoria on the other hand, didn't feel that same about him. She was still battling within herself. She had vowed to never allow herself to trust someone to the point that her life depended on it, like the first ordeal that almost cost her her life. However, in this situation, she felt empowered, because although she had been around the firing of a gun during New Years in the past, she never held a gun, yet alone owned her own personal deuce deuce.

In addition, he also had a sawed off shot gun in the duffle bag as well and wanted her to learn how to use them both. He had arranged for them to go to the gun range to get some lessons and let off some rounds at target practice. This feeling of protection was a feeling that she hadn't felt in a long time since she was a child. Victoria's uncle would teach her and her siblings how to box so she was an absolute fighter and an even more fierce diva that not only enjoyed boxing, but she loved playing and watching all sports. Now she could add gun owner and shooter to her resume, making her a real pistol! The thrill she got from shooting her gun and hitting the target on their weekend practices were exhilarating… and yet somewhat scary. She knew that if she was ever put in a position where she had to use a gun, she certainly would do it without hesitation. Now, back to the time when the two bullets came thru the window and Victoria's desire to move…

Within a week, Mr. Smooth had arranged for them to meet his realtor, Mr. Payton, who had already initiated negotiations for the purchase of a one-bedroom condo in the Capitol Hill area of Southeast DC. It was located within walking distance of Potomac Avenue subway station and blocks away from a familiar place that she visited on weekends as a child at least 3 – 4 times but it had been a long time since she had been back. Those visits would consist of visiting a family member with kids her age on the weekend. Her family members relocated to the Potomac Garden public housing from Uptown DC and lived in building 700, which was a high rise. Although it was fun and there were a lot of kids, the most memorable time was when Victoria got to sing a song by her favorite artist, Whitney Houston, in the summer talent show outside and everyone loved her voice, and she became very popular.

The last weekend of her visit there, she was made to stand in the corner as a family friend that was dating her family member, accused Victoria of telling their business to other family. Now at this time, Victoria was only eight years old and an innocent child. What she came to realize later on in life was that this person was hooked on drugs and never in their right state of mind. So that weekend of having to stand in the corner for hours with taps from a rubber flip flop along with yelling to the top of her lungs, in hindsight, made her realize that he was just talking out of his head. He later apologized for having an episode and let her know that he never would have done those things if he was in his right state of mind.

As Victoria reflected on her past life, she was excited about the opportunity to purchase her first condo and actually be a real estate owner. Only thing was that those visions of a new start in a new home were short lived, due to what happened on the day that they were moving into their condo. She realized that the first mistake that she made was agreeing to purchase the condo with a man that is not your husband. A powerful lesson that she learned from this situation was to never put a man's name in anything unless you were married, and you both were financially invested in the marriage and property. Well, getting back to the day of the move. It started out great as the moving truck was rented the night before, allowing the movers, that were hired friends and family of Mr. Smooth, to get an early start and have the truck fully loaded by 8:00 am for the first run, as the paperwork was signed the day before and the keys were already in their possession. By noon that day, they were fully moved in.

Victoria needed to go downtown to return the keys to the rental office. However, as she was preparing to leave and get in her vehicle double parked in the alleyway of her street, someone walked up, that lived in the neighborhood and knew Mr. Smooth. He introduced Victoria as his lady and told them to make sure everyone knew who she was, because she was off limits. Now, just as that conversation was finishing up, another guy walked up and began talking to Mr. Smooth just as the other friend left and kissed Victoria's hand to say nice to meet you. Well, that was a big mistake! Just as he was raising his head up, Mr. Smooth proceeded to open the car door while holding the guy's head in between the window and door. He smashed the guy head in the door at least three to four times, while telling him, "How dare you disrespect me while I'm standing right here!" I just told you that was my lady and she's off limits." The look in the guy eyes was that of fear and the look in Mr. Smooth eyes was that of pure evil.

Victoria realized then that the real psychopath had shown up and that smoothness was nothing more than an act. However, at this time the deal was done and there was nothing that she could do but withhold intimacy from him. At this point it had only been four months that they were together. During the next couple of months, Mr. Smooth was on the road with his trucking company, which allowed it to be easier for Victoria not to have to deal with him. He would only be home one day a week and every time he would get home, she would either go to the club or be asleep. In addition, as she found out a week after they moved into the condo, Mr. Smooth expressed to her that his mother had overdosed in a house a few feet away from their condo and that was also where she was found deceased. Ever since then, Mr. Smooth had started smoking PCP, which is phenyl cyclohexyl piperidine or a dissociative drug that causes people to have distorted perceptions due to the significant mind-altering effects. He also started smoking Marijuana joints, and she hated how it had begun to make him look and act. He had become so unattractive to her that she couldn't stand to look at him, yet alone allow him to touch her in a sexual way, which was why she avoided him for almost eight months.

During this time, she continued to do everything she could to enjoy her life, and although she had male friends, they were merely platonic relationships. Most guys were attracted to her because she enjoyed sports and life, and she never disrespected herself and honestly just didn't want to be with anyone. She had two really close male friends and one that she had known since she was about fourteen and was considered her protector. Since he was about four years older than she was, he would come to her defense against Mr. Smooth, that we'll get into shortly.

So, getting back to the fact that during her almost a year long relationship with Mr. Smooth, they literally lacked a sexual life besides him giving her cunnilingus (oral sex) which was more pleasurable for her, but she only allowed him to please her in the experience. It also meant that she didn't have to feel violated by her disgust of him. Ironically, though she still appreciated him being her protector and on occasions she recalls feeling reconnected to him, but it was always short lived, because when someone shows you who they are, she realized that she had to accept that he showed her the real Psychopath.

It was a Wednesday night, and every week Victoria would go to the Metro Club located on Bladensburg Road, in the District of Columbia. It looked like an abandoned building on the outside as it sat across the street from the Washington Area Metro Transit Bus lot that sat next to a liquor store. During her Wednesday night outings, she always primarily drove by herself, but met up with a few associates that also attended the same spot weekly. In fact, she had attended the club back in the day, before the entire car accident ordeal with one of her good girlfriends that introduced her to some associates of hers.

Well, getting back to the story, this one particular Wednesday, there was this guy at the club whose name was Bear. Every week, he would compliment Victoria on how nice she looked and especially since after the recovery time she had been away, he hadn't seen her, but wanted to get to know her. Well, Victoria was very off standish in the club when it came to the fellas, since they had nothing, she wanted or needed. Although Mr. Smooth was no longer attractive to her, she still respected him for always providing and protecting her. So, guys would often refer to her as "high maintenance", because they knew she was taken care of and was a classy lady. She was always dressed to impress, and also loved to dance, and at times danced very seductively.

She would often stand in the back and enjoy her space, while never allowing anyone to dance with her. So, on this night, the guy Bear became overly intrigued and apparently turned on by Victoria's sex appeal, that he decided to take a chance. However, as he approached her from behind and attempted to dance with her, she immediately turned around and told him to move away from her...and he complied as he thought it was a game of hard to get. Until he tried again, and he pulled her arm firm but seductively while saying "come here girl". At that moment, Victoria felt violated and disrespected. She became visibly upset, so much so that just as the club was about to close, she cursed him out and said, I have something for you. Bear begins to get embarrassed now, as people are starting to pay attention as they have never seen Victoria that upset or such an interaction between the two. Now as Victoria was getting ready to leave, she asked one of her female associates for her number, as she was friends with Bear and had known him for years from her significant other.

Victoria went home, flying down Seventeenth street and scurrying right onto Potomac Avenue as she ran the light to cross Pennsylvania Avenue to get there. To her surprise, Mr. Smooth was home asleep in the bed, as he said one of his ship-ments was canceled so he came home and would be there for the next two days. She proceeded to tell him what happened at the club and how disrespected she felt. In true Mr. Smooth fashion, he asked her if she wanted him to take care of him for her, and she said no, as she thought to herself, that she didn't want to have him killed. So, he tells her, well that's why I bought you the deuce deuce, but whatever you do, make sure you wear your clothes and go handle your business. I'm here if you need me. Well, that was all the confirmation that she needed, so she made a phone call to the associate, who provided the location, which was about a thirty-minute drive from her house. But with the adrenaline running through her veins, Victoria didn't care, all she knew was that she was on a mission to prove to this guy that she was not to ever be touched or disrespected. Upon her arrival, which was now about 4:00 am in the morning, as the club had let out at two, she pulled up and tapped the horn several times until his brother came outside pleading for her to leave. Victoria proceeds to tell him what happened and that his brother needed to come outside and apologize before she set the house on fire, which meant she would shoot her gun.

She didn't want to hurt Bear, but she wanted him to apologize and vow to never make that mistake again. After about twenty minutes, everyone was assured that she wasn't going to shoot, Bear came out and expressed his apology. This only made him become more enticed and intrigued as he stated that in her presence, that he had a lot of respect for her gangster as she stood there with her black gloves on, with the car running in the middle of the street with her gun on her side. From that day on, they became cool although he wished for more, but he knew that was never going to happen and he never crossed that line again, and she felt in part she owed that feeling of power to Mr. Smooth, reinforcing her ability to be fierce.

There was a second occasion at another time that she left the club, but this was on a Saturday, and it was a special event that she had purchased tickets for in advance in order to attend a GoGo event at the Icebox club. Now initially she would not have been there since she was in a car accident about 3 weeks prior in which someone ran a red light just as she was entering into the Freeway. The vehicle hit and her vehicle, spun around and ended up hitting a tree deploying the airbags and reinjuring her knee. So, while she was going through the process of getting her insurance matter resolved and feeling fearful yet again because of another car accident, she now needed another vehicle. Well, of course Mister Smooth always came through. Because she took the loss of her vehicle, he surprised her and bought them both "his and hers" 1988 Twin Turbo Z made by Nissan. Her car was candy apple red with the T top that everyone loved. Since she had minor bruises, it was recommended to wear a brace on her knee. After all of that, she was still able to go to the Ice Box show.

Lessons Learned: Situational awareness is critical for one's sustainability of life and never allow someone to violate you in any form. However, how you respond matters much more than what initiated the situation in the first place.

CHAPTER 9

Sweating Bullets

Now with regards to the incident that occurred that night was a moment in which Victoria was feeling very empowered, took on a battle that was not hers. After dealing with certain associates, she realized that a young girl named Dixie was in fact involved in a lot of negative situations, but Victoria always looked at this as moments of clarity if anyone that is in her presence is being disrespected. One particular night, there was a situation between the girl Dixie and some other females that were from North Carolina. As Victoria was leaving and headed to her car, Dixie and a couple of her other friends were all parked near Victoria's vehicle. These girls from North Carolina were talking disrespectfully to Dixie because they had been flirting with someone she liked. The girls from North Carolina repeatedly were talking about how they get down in Greensboro, as they began calling Victoria's associate A B!T?H.

Dixie never said anything, but she did attempt to laugh it off and ignore it until Victoria asked them to please stop calling her out her name. But they continued to call her out of her name along with other disrespectful names. At this point Victoria was fed up with the disrespect and felt that she needed to take matters into her own hands. Since Victoria always thought that she can do whatever she wanted, whenever she wanted, and to whomever she wanted, she told the girls that if they said another curse word again then they were gonna have a problem. Well of course these girls from North Carolina felt like they were from the down and Dirty South and unafraid, continued being disrespectful. Then Victoria, feeling like she had had enough, punched one girl in the mouth. That, of course, sparked an all-out brawl where everyone was fighting. Believe it or not, that had only been Victoria second time ever getting into any kind of fight.

Now you're probably wondering what this story has to do with Mister Smooth. Well, Victoria went home, and she told Mr. Smooth how she hit the girl in the face and all the details she could remember as to how they looked. No, it was not very ladylike at all especially since Victoria always knew that she had skills with boxing that many did not have, since she did not fight like the traditional girl with the swinging of the arms wildly and scratching at the face.

She also felt like it was her responsibility to defend the weak and never allow anyone to be bullied in her presence. And she also knew that if ever she needed a situation handled, then Mr. Smooth was always going to take care of it for her. So, of course when she told Mr. Smooth, he took action and ended up finding the girl some weeks later as the ladies had gone back to North Carolina. However, when they returned back to DC, he found the girl that actually hit Victoria, since he had someone stake out the nightclub every week, until they eventually returned to the club. And of course, he had that situation handled like a silver bullet and had one of his friends beat the girl up. Unfortunately, by the time he had someone to handle the situation, the drugs started impacting his life. He had resumed selling drugs and threatening people as he had got into an accident with his truck and so he was out of work. He needed to find an alternative, so he resorted to what he knew best and that was the street life.

However, that was not what Victoria was all about, and in fact, that was the straw that broke the camel 's back. She needed to move because she felt she could no longer take it. Fast forward to the time almost two months after the incident with the girls from North Carolina. Victoria had already devised her plan. She had already obtained an apartment and vowed that she would be moving soon. However, she needed to find someone or somewhere to stay temporarily until she could make that transition. But Mister Smooth was not having it.

Victoria was in the house one day in her lingerie cooking dinner, enjoying what she loves to do: cook, drink her wine, and relax to music. He had been gone for two days so on this particular night, Mr. Smooth had other plans, and when he walked in the door and saw Victoria in the silk gown that he had brought her months ago, but never wore for him. He often bought her random gifts and lingerie from Victoria's Secret. He wanted her and was still very much aroused by her. He asked her if they could have sexual relations and she immediately rejected him…telling him once again that he had become unattractive to her and that the drugs even had begun to affect his skin. He became enraged and proceeded to speak on the fact that she hadn't had sex with him in almost nine months and that he was always pleasing her. He spoke on the fact, that she had never even given him oral sex. Then he grabbed her and ripped her night gown. He was clearly high on drugs and told her that either she gives him some sex, or he was going to take it!

At this point he was willing to take it because she was his woman and to him that wouldn't be considered rape. Victoria managed to run into the kitchen and get a butcher's knife, but at this point, the knife seemed insignificant, because he had now pulled out his gun and placed it to her head. Ironically, even though she was sweating bullets, she wasn't scared and told him, "Well one of us is going to die tonight, because you not getting nothing from me." The expression on his face was clearly one of shock and surprise. That moment made him laugh and lower the gun. Just as he did that, she made her great escape, pushed him and ran out the front door and down the stairs of her condo going to her car. Although the car was unlocked, she realized that she had left her keys in the house. Shortly thereafter, he came down the stairs, dangling the key and walking to the driver's side of the car, telling her to get out. Now, he wasn't going to make a scene outside because to the streets, he was the man everybody was afraid of, and Victoria was his woman, and he didn't want to appear weak. So, as he opened the car door on the driver's side, he grabbed her by the neck and punched Victoria.

But shortly thereafter his friend appeared. He knew he couldn't allow his friend to see him in a state of disdain and disrespect to women since he had portrayed the image of a man that cared about and loved his mother. Although she had been deceased for some time, he also adored his sisters that were from various mothers, but the same father. He always loved and protected them in public. So, in the moment of all that chaos, he stepped away from the vehicle. And just as he proceeded to move away Victoria grabbed the keys, started the car and zoomed down the street, however she didn't get far because she realized at the moment she needed to go back and get some things.

She circled the block going down and around Potomac Avenue to come back through K Street. As she peered through the island to see if she had seen him, he was no longer in sight. Victoria knew that this was her time to grab some things and to take flight. But lo and behold he was waiting and lurking too. He started walking around as if he predicted or knew that she would return. Then when it seemed that she had a few moments, she ran upstairs and grabbed some things and then proceeded to come back down. Then she saw him, and he grabbed her and started hitting her. He threw her in the car and threatened to set her hair on fire if she resisted, while he flicked the lighter that he already had in his hand. At that point she just moved over in the vehicle on the passenger side attempting to flee, terrified for her life on a beautiful summer night that quickly turned ugly. He grabbed the door from within the car and slammed it. The very next punch would really be a blow that hurt her. She then made up her mind at that moment to look like she had given up.

She decided to be still and appeared to be unconscious, not allowing him to know that she was planning her great escape. He climbed over her and got in the driver's side of the vehicle as he then drove off hurrying down Pennsylvania Avenue on to the Susan Bridge and onto the freeway so they could get up to 495 towards Virginia. Just as Victoria looked up, she realized that she had no clue as to where they were going, as it was like they were on a roller coaster ride. It looked like cars were zooming by going almost 100 mph and in the midst of it she remained calm and slumped over as he then proceeded to feel for her pulse on her arm, but she remained lifeless allowing her arm limb to just fall as if she was out of it and completely unconscious.

Sweating bullets, she peered out the window, while raising her head slightly, within minutes after they were driving, so that she could get an idea of her location, to flee whenever she would get a chance. As they were speeding down the highway there was a loud boom, and she knew at that time they had been in an accident, but she didn't know to extent what the impact was. Fortunately for her, they hit a curb and the airbag deployed right on her back as she was slumped over. The car spun out onto the highway. He jumped out and got on the passenger side with the car facing southbound to oncoming traffic as he opened the door so that he could check her pulse. Victoria made a moan, so that he became aware that she was not dead.

At that moment, two people came up who had seen the incident because they were impacted by the hit. They checked on her and she immediately arose and said, "Please take me, I gotta go I can't be with him", so they asked her if she was hurt, and she said, "Yes, please, I gotta go, don't leave me here just take me". They offered to take her to a hospital. They all got into the couple's Pathfinder or maybe a Range Rover and as they drove, he told them to please take us to the hospital in DC. The nearest hospital would have been the great DC General, known to those of low income but the emergency that was always willing to accept and take on trauma patients at no expense. And yet this was a place that she knew would be a safe haven for her. As they arrived at the hospital entrance, he kept telling her grasping and squeezing her hand whispering, "You better not say anything if you say anything I will kill you." They looked at her, they saw the fear and terror in her eyes they asked her if she was gonna be okay or if there anyone they could call.

At that time all Victoria could say was "No, please just let me out at the front door and wait until I go into the entrance" and they did just so they waited until she walked in and was at the emergency room clerk desk awaiting to be seen. She was no doubt battered and bruised from the position that she laid in the car really had her tumbling around in the front with a twisted ankle as well as other issues. Mr. Smooth snuck off in the wind. He left her since he was near his main area and feared that she just might tell the police.

With him being a convicted and former felon that had no fear of authority and had no value for life. He left in that moment because unbeknownst to her, he was coming back for a moment that could potentially take her life if she did not remain his woman. During this time many hours would pass before she could even have visitors. But she knew that it was a matter of life and death. She stayed for about 5 hours. She was given crutches and some medication for the pain. She sustained minor head injury, neck and back, as well as various bruises from the assault.

Unfortunately, there was no one that she could call immediately because all of her family was still out of town except for her brother who was younger than her but was always there whenever she needed him. Victoria called him and got a ride in a cab to his home. She stayed with him for a few days to recuperate to be there when the family came back home. She worked on her next plan of action to figure out where she would go and what she would do.

She knew that staying at the condo that they purchased together was no longer going to be an option for her but would only work if he was no longer there. Within 2 weeks she had remained away from him without any contact. She changed her cell phone number so that he could not have any means to contact her. As crazy as it was, he knew that he couldn't contact her mom or any members of her family because no one liked him and so he must wait it out not just going around different areas anticipating if she would even come to the condo. As time went by, she knew she just needed to make herself a complete exit from him.

This was a pivotal moment in her life, and she could only rely on God and her friends. One friend in particular had always been supportive in giving advice and so one particular day they went out as they normally would to watch a basketball game with some friends. She just got her mind off of things and never would have imagined that at that moment their lines of friendship would be blurred. That ended up being the greatest game and the best time she ever had.

As the months went by, it had almost been 2 months. So, she went back to her place to gather some things as by this time she had already found a new home in the Northeast area. However, just as she was going back home, Mr. Smooth appeared on a bike in the parking lot where her mom resided. He pulled out a gun and said, "Yeah I've been waiting for you, and you need to come with me or I'm going to kill you." She was able to run back into the building and to make a call to her good friend who had always been her protector for many years. Within the next 20 minutes her friend appeared and immediately he pulled up. Old Mr. Smooth was still circling around on a bicycle like the psychopath and lunatic he was. Victoria's friend opened the truck and gathered his two guns and asked Victoria to come outside. Mr. Smooth looked in a state of shock because he had never expected this little Uptown girl to bring force against the infamous Southeast Enforcer. But her friend came with all the smoke ready to blow some major deuce deuce holes if necessary. Well, Mr. Smooth recognized that he was definitely unmatched and that he could not win at this moment. He said he'll be back and rolled off on his bike.

A few weeks would go by, and Victoria started to gradually feel better and ready to resume her life. She knew that she needed to leave her job. Fortunately, she was just working as a temp and so she asked for a new location somewhere so that he would not be able to locate her. This ended up being in Alexandria, Virginia. She had already been maintaining her funds, so she was able to purchase another vehicle. She would ensure that again she could reign as Victoria, the woman that became resilient in the face of danger even when life threatened her, even after betrayed by someone that didn't know how to love, even after being with someone that was an abuser, even after being with someone that was hiding his true identity.

So, from all this drama she learned to never rush into anything and to be observant and proceed with caution, and most importantly follow your instincts. She recalled that day she met him, thinking that it was going to be a scary ride. She remembered that he immediately gave her stalker vibes especially when he called her phone just moments after receiving the phone number. Nonetheless Victoria knew that it was yet another moment in her life that she had been given a second chance to overcome and become victorious in everything else that she did.

Lessons Learned: Strategic planning, critical thinking along with wisdom and determination are skills that are needed when somebody shoots at you in a way that can impact your life. Seeking help on the road to recovery is a way to finally win back your life.

CHAPTER 10

A Straight Shooter

Victoria knew that only time would tell, before she knew exactly what her next chapter would be. At this moment she had no expectations on love and just wanted to live her life carefree with no attachments and no men in her life. She just wanted to travel the world and embrace herself getting back into the things that she knew were best for her: the Bible, her education, and participating in community engagement events. She wanted to get back to the things that fulfilled her. She knew that this rebranding would bring a new appreciation for herself, and that the revamped Victoria knew that she needed a plan. One that would be monumental, impactful and meaningful in her life now.

Victoria loved doing hair. She went back to cosmetology school and completed her hours. It was fulfilling. It had been a family trade and as time went on, she even considered going into a shop, but then realized that she didn't want that kind of responsibility, she just loved doing hair as a hobby. She never really learned how to do braiding though. She just stuck to mastering the art of hair coloring.

About two months after she completed her program, Victoria became very sick. It was something that she hadn't experienced since the last car accident. She was working on her health and always made sure that she lived a healthy lifestyle. She used weight supplements to gain weight. She worked out with a personal trainer. She was always a thin girl looking like a "Barbie" with the hourglass shape that everyone wanted. So, to suddenly become this ill was something that Victoria never expected would happen again. She knew that this was something that she needed to deal with immediately. Her game plan did not include contingencies for becoming sick because she worked two jobs. She liked very nice things that cost a lot of money and she had learned her lesson not to depend upon a man to be the supplier of those things, so she needed to be independent. She also learned that when you do have someone that truly supports you, it's not one-sided but it's a partnership.

With the new location of her home being in Northeast, it was still new to her and with the pain so excruciating, she knew that despite the fact that DC General was the hospital for those that were needy, her experience with them gave her a fond appreciation for the possibilities. She was optimistic that although they were in the hood, they had great doctors that could help her to identify and resolve whatever sickness she was experiencing.

Victoria hopped into her new 1997 Mazda 626 sedan and drove herself to the hospital. The time that she sat in the waiting room was unbearable. It was unbelievable how long it took. During the wait she began to think about her new friend that she started to take very seriously. Although they were considering it, there was some hesitancy since she had experienced so many bad situations that she knew that she did not want to ever get involved in it again. When she finally got seen by the doctor, she shared with them her symptoms. In the next few hours Victoria received so many different tests but they all were negative. Finally, they decided to give her a sonogram since that was the only thing that they had not done because there was no reason to ever check to see if she was pregnant.

They saw the medical history and the records from the hospital from her accident stating that conception was impossible, and that the percentage was so low that that was a last thought on their mind. When they put the sonogram instrument on her stomach and proceeded to swab over her with the roller from side to side the doctor said "Ohhh... I see what is happening." The doctor turned the screen to her and said this is what I'm talking about. This is what is causing all of the pain". Victoria felt lost and confused, feeling incompetent because she did not know what was on the screen. Then the doctor said this is your baby girl! She looked and said "What!? No that's impossible! They said I can't have any children." Then the doctor said, "All things are possible!" That reality was a game changer for Victoria as the impossible became possible and would forever change her life as she firmly believed that children were gifts from God, and this was the blessing that she needed.

Victoria stared at the screen and asked for a blood test to confirm it. But the doctor offered to do something even better. She turned up the volume on the sonographer machine and allowed her to hear the heartbeat of her own unborn child within her at the prime age of 20 weeks. Victoria was blown away! 20 weeks would have been 4 months. She had no clue that she was pregnant. She also knew that the blurred lines moment with her friend was her only means of getting pregnant. She also knew that her current friendship was another situation of impossibilities because he said the doctor said that he was infertile.

Now, imagine this… if you know a guy and a girl who had been friends for a few years decided to get together and the unimagined happens. Then he goes on but there is another friend who steps up in the row and he himself was told that he couldn't have any kids. Immediately Victoria knew she had to have a conversation. She made the call in the phone booth in the hospital. Her cell phone wasn't working back in those days and Wi-Fi didn't exist, so she called from the phone booth and told her friend and all he could say was "Wow! Are you sure? Do you think it's mine? And she said "Well, I've only had one other situation, but we were protected and that was way before we really decided to see each other so you must be the "straight shooter." This leg of Victoria's journey has yet again given her another shot at life. This time, in a room of love that would breed love…and make a new life.

And, oh, about Mr. Smooth. It wasn't long before he went on a rampage trying to find Victoria, and when he found her, he busted through the window where she lived. Good thing she was smart enough to get bars on her window in the apartment because she knew he threatened to kill her. We will talk about that story next. But for now, we will close this chapter reflecting on the fact that there are moments when death and fear seems to be inevitable, but faith and resilience can be a lifesaver.

Lessons Learned: Victoria learned that wisdom and determination are skills that are needed when shots are fired, and that seeking recovery is always the winner.

CHAPTER 11

A Shot at a Second Chance...
Motherhood

Now that the news that Victoria was becoming a mother had started to set in, she was still in disbelief as she left the hospital. All she could think about was what do I do now? She reminisced about the scenario that she had with her good friend, and also the recent relationship that she had been in flooded her mind. But all that really mattered was that she was blessed and given a second chance to be a mother. But this time was different because she never thought about really loving anyone other than herself. She knew that she had already seen the type of mother how not to be, and in this moment all she could think about was the type of mother that she wanted to be and how much she needed not only her mother, but also her father who had not been involved in her life as much as she wanted.

Victoria went home trying to make sense of it all, trying to figure out exactly what her next steps would be. While trying to figure out how all this could even be possible. She thought about all the times that she had dyed her hair two or three different times in a night and how she still had a menstrual cycle every month, and how much she drank when she would go out to the club. She never considered how it would impact her baby.

At this point, the reality was setting in that she was in fact going to be someone's mother. She was given the due date of July 4th. Initially all she thought of was how she was going to party and be a mother. She was quickly approaching five months and reflected on the loss of her unborn child less than three years ago, as a result of that near fatal car accident, and fact that she was told that she would not ever be able to have any children.

And now, to be blessed with the real possibility of being a mother, this would change Victoria's life forever. She meditated deeply on her next steps and life trajectory. Over the next few days, Victoria reflected on all the events that happened in her life. Planning for the welcoming of her child became a pivotal point in her life. She wanted to reach out and rectify situations in her relationships. The first one was that she needed to have a conversation with, was with her mother.

As you recall, Victoria's mother was absent from her life growing up dealing with her addiction. There were times that she intervened or was there on the weekend, but despite all of that the most defining moment was when her mom came to her bedside when she was fighting for her life. She was only three days clean, and her mother never looked back. Victoria realized that at that moment, all she wanted was to be Mommy's little girl. So she had arranged to meet with her on a nice sunny day in the park in Uptown DC. Her mother agreed but Victoria had not yet shared the wonderful news which would be a surprise.

Immediately upon telling her mother that she was going to be a mother, her mom said I'm glad that you shared this with me, and I would love to have a chance to be in my grandchild 's life. I apologize for not being there in yours. The lesson that Victoria learned in this moment was how wonderful forgiveness could be and how great it was to live a life free of grudges and regrets. She told her mother "I will give you my promise that during the first year after having my child I will live with you."

This was an experience that neither of them knew what to expect but they knew that this was something that they both wanted and that they would never regret. In hindsight, it really motivated them to build the bond between themselves for their sake, and most importantly for this young precious life that was soon to come into the world. At the time, Victoria's mother lived Uptown on 13th place in DC. Having just went through the ordeal with Mr. Smooth, the psychopath and breaking in, the timing was impeccable.

Victoria moved in with her mother. Then, shortly there-after her mom purchased a home in which they could all be together. This was a highlight for Victoria because she got to be a little girl in a woman's body. Having her mother at her side was something that she didn't realize that she even needed, but yet she really longed for. It was an experience that was fulfill-ing emotionally and allowed her to accept and receive uncon-ditional love from her mother. It also allowed her mother to be able to give and feel complete within herself. So much so that she went through her recovery programs without any drugs. Her mom soon became her best friend.

Interestingly, what this also did was make Victoria want to really have a better relationship with her father. As the months progressed, Victoria was fast approaching six months of preg-nancy and now had to plan a baby shower. She put behind her all the hurtful things that reminded her of her painful upbringing. She remembered the good things about how she loved watching Sesame Street, and how she also loved and enjoyed watching cartoons. She decided to make her baby shower theme Looney Tunes. Planning the shower was incredibly fulfilling for Victoria and healing at the same time.

Now things were starting to get interesting because first she was told that she was having a girl, but by the time she was six months she was told that she was having a boy, so the Looney Tunes theme would be just perfect for a girl or a boy. She said at this point in her life the blessing was just to be able to have a baby. She had never really given it much thought because her life had been so dismal up to that point. She never imagined that she would really embrace her new reality to have a true second chance of not only being a mother but embracing being a daughter.

This moment allowed her mother and father to be in her life and in the life of her child. This was truly an amazing epiphany and evidence of her faith that things happen in due time and some things are just not in our control. But it also heightened her awareness of creation and how amazing her God was, and this was yet another defining moment in her life where she knew that she owed her Creator ultimately everything. That meant that it was time for her to give her life to God. This was something that she would have to pray about because there were things that needed to be adjusted in order to get on the right track of serving her God.

As time passed, when Victoria reached out to her father, she's already gained almost 60 pounds during this pregnancy and became an unimaginable weight. She had always been a very petite young woman from childhood, never wearing more than a size 6 as an adult. She was shapely but still very petite so having gained all this weight was an issue for her, but she didn't realize then it was just about being pregnant. In the last couple of months, she knew she had to make amends, which is why she reached out to her dad only to find out that within the next month he was moving to Atlanta. She pleaded with her father.

She remembered the moment she knocked on his door in Northeast DC standing there very much pregnant. He was surprised to see his daughter, but not only to see her, but to see her with child. She started to tear up and cry because she felt the little girl coming out in her. She realized she longed for her daddy. She never knew how much she needed him because Victoria only allowed herself to be strong, self-confident, and ambitious and never vulnerable. She was hard working and very intelligent, and beautiful. She never allowed her feelings to surface and never allowed herself to feel the pain that comes with abandonment. She had suppressed all these issues and consequently she never allowed herself to really live and thoroughly enjoy life.

Her father was a man that did not know his biological father and had only met him one time in his life, so he knew how his daughter felt. He knew that he could not leave and go to Atlanta at this moment when his baby girl needed him the most. He decided that he would stay in DC.

The interesting dynamic in this situation was he was leaving one situation to go and live with his girlfriend who had just recently relocated. They were expecting him to go and be married, but in this moment both her father's girlfriend and her dad understood that they had to be selfless and that there were some things that needed to be mended before they could move on. No doubt Victoria appreciated her father's decision to stay as he had come into her life again at another pivotal moment to be there for his daughter.

This was unconditional love given by her father. This is what she had needed in her life. This is what she had wanted but did not realize that she needed. This was similar to when he had to trust and believe in her and love her enough and to stand by her and her belief to make a decision not to get her a blood transfusion when her life was at stake. The moments that they encountered that day were significant enough to replace any negative feelings that she ever had for him because nothing that he had done in the past mattered anymore. He had shown up and he was present at those critical moments that she needed him the most. Needless to say, these were life changing and transformational periods in her life.

Lessons Learned: The lessons she learned was that it taught her that this is what a man is supposed to do. It showed her that all men are not dogs that all men are not selfish. The journey in life is never an easy one. It's one that is challenging and that has unforeseen nuances and occurrences, but trauma can always be defeated by love.

CHAPTER 12

The Silver Bullet

Although Victoria's life may have been daunting, the most beautiful thing was about to happen to her. In this moment, she felt renewed and was able to give birth to a beautiful handsome baby boy who was a godsend in her life. This event furthered her understanding of what it meant to have unconditional love for someone. The baby was born, and she named him Victor which was the male version of her name.

It's interesting how people say there's no handbook on being a parent and although that may be true, when Victoria found out that she was going to be a mother she obtained a book called "What To Expect When You're Expecting." She realized that the book could tell her how she would feel in that a particular month which was a true experience for her. She believed that life was a series of moments, And living was what you did with those moments. And what a grand moment it was because she was able to have her mom and her grandmother in the room with her while she gave birth to her son, 7 pounds and 6 ounces, with a fair complexion, and whose hair laid down on his head like a beautiful silk bonnet. He had the most perfect feet and hands and the most beautiful smell of a newborn baby.

In the moments during her pregnancy Victoria would anticipate and read everything that happened as she wrote daily in her journal. She wished that she would have been fully engaged and aware from the time she could feel her baby grow within her womb. Victoria knew that she needed to adjust her lifestyle. Her child's father was cooperative and after discussing it, they decided to give being together a try since they were just good friends trying to see where things were gonna' go. It was great in the beginning, but even the best of friends and the best intentions to do the right thing doesn't always mean it's the right thing to do. Victoria and her son's father decided that they didn't have to be together to take care of their son. They decided that they can co-parent. They didn't have any major issues or arguments besides the fact that she still wanted to go to the club. But because he worked and she worked, they just needed to figure out how they could be a family without being in a committed relationship, allowing each other to freely go on with their lives. They agreed that they could be with others as long as it was always understood that their child came first, and whomever came along would also have to respect that their child was a part of their life.

During the first two years of baby Victor's life, he was able to stay with his dad's babysitter, which was his aunt. They continued to give the love and nourishment, emotionally, mentally, and physically to their child at these very pivotal times of his life. In those first few years, they knew it was critical for the child to be taught in an environment that was conducive to enhanced development and that is exactly what happened.

By the time little Victor turned three, Mr. Smooth, the Psychopath, returned. He had gone to jail because he had gotten so high and had gotten so upset with her that he crashed the cars that he had bought for them. He bought her another vehicle to replace the one that he crashed, but of course he came in, and he took that back and crashed that up too! Then he went on a rampage with someone that was supposed to have been close to him, to the point that he bashed his head in nearly killing him. He was on a hunt to find Victoria, and somehow had evaded the police because he had gone out of town to Virginia. Some friends thought he was incarcerated but in fact was not. What resulted was his arrest when The United States marshals came to his house which was their old home on K Street. As a result, they were able to determine that Victoria was his last known girlfriend. Upon determining this, they started to do research by going through her motor vehicle records to get her last known address, which she always maintained as her childhood address Uptown.

On one very early Friday morning there is a bang at her grandmother's door but she's not there. But she's told what had happened because the police and the US marshals were on the roof adjacent and across from the house with guns and rifles drawn pointing at her grandparents asking for Victoria's whereabouts as well as that of Mr. Smooth. Victoria's grandmother had no knowledge because she had not spoken to him in years. He had gotten really weird because she would get calls with an error code 000 phone number 000000 and she had not a clue as to who it was. But she would later find out that in fact it was the FBI. Ohhh… they were definitely on his line looking for him. They even started tapping her phone because somehow because she had always stayed in contact with his sister who was fighting for her life with a critical disease because she felt sorry for her.

She had given her the phone number that in turn allowed her to be contacted by Mr. Smooth and unbeknownst to her, her phone was being tapped, so the police had already notified her and her grandparents of the situation.

When Victoria's grandmother finally connected with him, he told her that he needed to turn himself in and that he needed to speak to Victoria so that he could ask her a question in front of his face because he really could not understand how, as much as he had wanted a baby, why she didn't allow him to be the father of her child. And, as much as he wanted to try to be the child 's father, he bought him all these gifts and he just wanted to bring them to her. Well, she thought about it. The police contacted her told her you can go ahead. They said if you could try to talk to him, and we'll narrow down the location, and give him a chance to turn himself in.

Mr. Smooth told her that once he was able to bring the gifts to her that he was gonna turn himself in, so Victoria and her grandmother met him in southeast near where they used to have their apartment at his grandmother 's house. He pulled up and they got into the vehicle. They were talking as he was helping with the gifts, and he did have plenty of clothes and shoes and all types of other things for the baby. It looked like he must have spent at least a couple of $1,000.00 on large items and things for the baby. But after a few moments when she was in his presence, he started to get infuriated.

She knew then that it was time to go, but before he would allow her to leave, he said "I should just kill you right now!" And then he said, "But I'm not gonna do that, but I should burn your pretty face up" and he proceeds to take out his lighter and tries to set her hair on fire! Unbelievable! He was really trying to really take her out! She was able to open her door and yell and scream and flee as her grandmother and his grandmother came out telling her to just leave and for him to leave her alone. That would be the last time that she saw him, because shortly thereafter he was arrested and received 20 years in prison. The irony was she felt sorry for him because in the next few days before he would leave, she felt that she owed it to him to allow him to taste her one more time... It was a dismal thought for her, but she felt that she had ruined him and misled him because she was being selfish, and her actions really destroyed the man who had all intentions to be a very good person.

This silver bullet was betrayal at its finest that ultimately had destroyed him. It is a hardening shot to anyone, but you have to learn to forgive and to let go to move on to and to rebuild your life. That was the opportunity that she had to put all the negative feelings that she had in her life aside, and to just love on her son, and that's what she did. This made her want more children and that's when she met the deceiver.

Lessons Learned: Always pay attention to your health and well-being. The greatest gift was to be a mother to her child. Never give up hope because when it's your turn…it's your turn, so be ready to show up by pouring into yourself and extending grace to others.

CHAPTER 13

The Gravestone Tattoo

Victoria kept her commitment to live with her mother for one year as she said she would. But once her son was born, she moved a few blocks further north of where she had grown up. The area that she grew up in was close to mid-Northwest on Allbody Street Northwest. Within a year's time Victoria became aware of the fact that working in Maryland was too far and she needed to work closer to home. She got a new job that her aunt had recommended. Her new job was relatively close to her home and her mother was able to watch her son in the evenings. Even though Victoria enjoyed mothering she still very much enjoyed going out and making time for herself and now she had a live-in babysitter.

By this time Victoria had her new vehicle and every evening upon arriving from work she would notice a gentleman that would be outside in his work suit. During this time, Victoria was also introduced to an associate named Shakena, that later turned into a snake from which she would learn valuable lessons …to be discussed later. Shakena was from Atlanta and lived most of her teen years in Silver Spring, Maryland. She shared a mutual friend with Victoria. Over time, Shakena and another friend, Chira would often see Victoria at the clubs, and on some occasions. They would carpool in to GoGo events outside of the District.

On one summer afternoon, Victoria saw Rizzo, who was a Puerto Rican prince, with light brown skin, and dark fine hair like that of waves in an ocean. The only problem was he was all about the streets. Upon seeing Rizzo, when Victoria was being dropped off by Shakena, she suddenly felt like this was the moment to showcase her skills and boom…that's when the bet was made. She proceeded to tell Shakena that she was willing to bet her $100 that she could get Rizzo off that corner and make him fall in love with her within thirty days.

The deal was done, the bet was made, and the game was on. So, one day Victoria had just come from the GoGo and was dressed to the tee with her bodycon halter top with her white shorts and her red heels. Her natural beauty was enhanced with some popping lip gloss. At this time Victoria's son was less than a year old. She had cut her hair close and colored it fiery red or even more appropriately, the color was called "Red Hot". Victoria knew that when she stepped out of the car, it was as if she was on fire. He always looked at her and was always very respectful. He always said hello and always watched her as she walked to the door. On this particular day she decided that she would give Rizzo some conversation. Upon getting out of the vehicle, as usual Rizzo said hello and she replied, "Hello Rizzo how are you?" They had previously exchanged names since they had seen each other for a few months now.

As the conversation went on, Victoria asked Rizzo a very intriguing, yet endearing question. She said, "You really look like a hard-working man. I'm quite sure the woman in your life who makes sure that you're always taken care of. Or is that not the case?" Rizzo, now listening very closely, stands straight up away from the gate he was leaning on, with his blue jumpsuit that looked like he had just got off work, says to her "I don't have a woman, Mama. I'm just a man out here trying to make it, making sure I take care of my family." So, Victoria then says, "Ohhh, then that would explain why you're always out here leaning on the gate. Is this the only pastime that you have because you stay out here very late." Rizzo then replied, "I just like being outside. I go to work every day and go check on my mother to make sure she's good and I come outside and go back in." Victoria acknowledges what he says with a nod and then says, "Go back in?" He then says, "Yes, I live around the corner. I have a condo and my mom is visiting with me for a couple of months because she was sick."

Well in that moment the curiosity really rose because Victoria wanted to see just what type of man Rizzo really was. When she finally finished talking to him, she really enjoyed the conversation and that started the challenge. A few days later she saw Rizzo again and this particular evening she was bringing in some groceries, so Rizzo came over and assisted her with the groceries. She said suggestibly, "Well maybe one day I'll give you a plate of food because I've never seen you eat anything out here. Rizzo smiled and said that sounds really good, but I only eat certain types of food and before I would even allow you to cook, I think you should go with me to my favorite restaurant, so you have a sense of what I like." Then, Victoria said to Rizzo, "Are you asking me on a date because it surely sounds like you are". So he asks in a joking way with a big smile, "I suppose I am, are you going to tell me no?" Victoria smiled and she said, "Well, I don't just go to just any type of restaurants, so if you are a Red Lobster type of guy, that's not me." She smiled and laughed, but she was very serious. In that moment, they both agreed that they definitely were not Red Lobster type of people and that there's nothing wrong with Red Lobster because they both loved the garlic-cheese biscuits! She was more of a steak and lobster type of girl and so he also agreed that he also loved steak and seafood too.

So, for the next week or so they continued on with the small talk and flirts. Then it proceeded to her coming out on the stoop and him coming over and talking to her for hours about life and things, their expectations, and what family meant to them. As a result, they got to know each other better. And then it happened -- the date to Del Frisco's and they had a great time. He picked her up in his Corvette! Now mind you, she had never seen his vehicle because he was always standing outside. She was very impressed that he was driving a Corvette. At this time, she still had her Mazda but then decided to buy her a Lexus. During the date, they had a great conversation. They ate good. They were in Crystal City, and they didn't want the night to end, so they even went to a movie, which was very unexpected.

He dropped her off at her vehicle and then he went about his way. The night ended around midnight and then they talked on the phone for an additional fifteen minutes while she got herself ready for bed. Then it started… the great conversation and additional dates was what they had looked forward to. By week three they were communicating regularly. She found out that he was working at a place in Greenbelt. He would text her often and just call to say hello. It was the little things. She was starting to become smitten by him and she was also starting to fall much harder than she had thought.

By the month's end, he had taken her to meet his mother and his mom confirmed that he never brought anyone home to meet her. Over the next two months, things were pretty much the same: dates, conversations, laughs, and just hanging out and having fun. By the third month, she had already of course won the bet and things looked hopeful, but they were happening very fast. By this time, it was going into the Fall and now her son is over a year old, and they were looking for a place to be together. She had agreed to one year and her mother had just purchased a home that was located in downtown northwest. Victoria was also looking for a home to purchase and wanted to ensure that she would have a chance to give her son an opportunity to grow up in a house just like the one she had grown up in. After a few months, she found a place but after six months with Rizzo, things had really become heated, in a great way. She thought maybe one day he would propose to her. He had always stated that he was a single man and that he had no longer been married because his wife had died. Victoria had no reason to doubt him because he did, in fact, have a tattoo of gravestone on his arm which stated, "Till death do us part Rizzo and Cora" with prayer hands underneath that stated, "Rest in Peace."

Lessons Learned – Betting on gambling with someone's life is like betting on the lottery expecting a guaranteed win, when the odds are a million to one.

CHAPTER 14

A Backfired Plan – He Wasn't Shooting Blanks

Victoria no doubt felt Rizzo's pain because he seemed genuinely sincere. He was very charismatic, and he had a heart of gold. He was very generous, and by now he had met her son, and was very involved and engaged with him. He would even pick him up from the daycare for her. As time progressed and the winter months rolled around, they were now looking for a home together. Everything was so blissful that they hoped that the birth of their next child would be together. So, what do you know, that in the months to come, they would have twin boys! Wow! It was so amazing and unbelievable at the same time. That they would be able to have two beautiful sons at once seemed unbelievable to Victoria because she had never thought that she would have kids. And going from having one son, and now to having three and possibly the idea of getting married, was never a thought that she ever had.

But one day this became a reality when a pretty ring was placed on her finger. They were out at dinner and enjoying each other 's company and unbeknownst to her he had asked the chef to prepare a special dessert for her however she didn't eat dessert. He had to make sure that it was something that she would be willing to try so he actually made a heart-shaped cookie that sat on a pear-shaped saucer. And lying on the side was a cinnamon twist that had the engagement ring on there. Victoria was blown away! They were only eighteen months into their relationship, and he was ready to propose. During the next few months after having the twins, Victoria remained with her mom until they were able to secure a place to live which ended up being outside of the city.

Unfortunately, Rizzo had gotten into some trouble, and he had gotten arrested for owing child support, and the crazy thing was he had only mentioned that he had a daughter and a son that both resided in the District of Columbia. However, that wasn't the case as he actually had an older daughter named Savanah who lived in North Carolina. In addition, it turned out that he had only been home a year after doing a ten-year prison bid, which he hadn't disclosed to Victoria. At this point, she realized that there were holes in the story that needed to be filled, and she needed to reevaluate the nature of their relationship because things just weren't adding up.

Just as things were starting to become even more questionable, Victoria discovered that she was pregnant again. She toiled with the decision of termination but finally decided to carry on with the pregnancy as there was a previous instance that she made such a decision that she regretted. So, at this point, Victoria began to reflect on her life and how she didn't want to be like her female associates that she knew were in abusive relationships after being cheated on or settling to deal with a guy, because the female was uneducated and unable to take care of herself financially and relying on someone other's income.

In that moment Victoria realized that her bet had back-fired because she basically had met Satan's son…the deceiver! It turned out that Rizzo wife wasn't dead at all, but in fact, she was very much alive and had also given birth to a set of twins a few months after Victoria's sons were born. Now this was indeed a painful blow not only to her emotionally, but also to her future as the man that she thought she won, actually dealt her a fatal blow. Upon finding out about his wife, when she went to pay his bail, only to have another woman sitting in the lobby yelling "So you're Victoria? I've been waiting to meet you as I've heard all about you. Victoria then asked… "and you are?" The woman then says, I'm Rizzo wife! To say she was devastated and surprised was an understatement. And, if that wasn't shocking enough, the woman then said… "Oh, I see why he's with you… you're definitely pretty, but this is what he does, he leaves home for a while, but always comes back. Except, this time he's got kids, so I needed to come see who this other woman was that my husband loves." Standing in a state of speechlessness, in a state of shock, Victoria continued to stare as her mind raced as she thought about her sons, the wedding plans, their unborn child and how Rizzo use to always say, "If I knew then, what I know now, things would be very different." Those words continued to be on repeat in her head and she finally knew what he meant, and suddenly became enraged. The irony of it all was that the day before was Christmas, and Victoria had spent all day with   Rizzo's mother, stepfather, and their kids at his parents' new house.

Just then, Rizzo was being released and came out of lock-up. He immediately, walked over to Victoria and asked the wife, "Why are you here? You need to just sign the divorce papers, because we're done and have been." As they walked outside to their cars, the wife was parked next to Victoria car. It was later revealed that Rizzo had driven the car to take his kids with the wife to the doctor. Interestingly, the wife responded to Rizzo with the signed divorced papers that she retrieved out of the car, as she said, "I'll see you in court."

On the ride home, Victoria and Rizzo had a crucial conversation laying all the cards on the table…so she thought. Following her heart and not her head. Since they already had a family trip to Hawaii planned with her family for a week-long vacation, she forgave Rizzo. Now at this point in her life, she's just shy of turning twenty-four and realizes that she is in love with the wrong man. The lesson for all is when you're young and in love, being blind and naive and living life as a façade is very deceptive. You have to learn to be truthful to yourself and see and accept the writing on the wall and walk away from manipulative situations. But Victoria didn't do that. For a few months things seemed normal, and he was even bringing the other twins over to the house once a month. Within a year, Victoria gave birth to her fourth child.

One night, Rizzo wasn't answering the phone very late at night. And by this time, Victoria was dealing with post-partum depression that was heightened by her woman's intuition. She felt something deep in her gut that something wasn't right. She knew that this wasn't a normal feeling and that a real situation was about to unfold. After several times calling Rizzo without getting any response, not even a text returned, Victoria got her boys together and put them in the car as she drove to his wife's house. They were able to be cordial with one another for the sake of the kids and therefore knew where each other lived.

Upon arrival Victoria did not see Rizzo 's car so she got in front of the house and started to beep the horn loudly and repeatedly! Mind you, it was at least 11:00 pm at night and fortunately all the kids were asleep, but she knew something was not quite right. After 10 minutes of her blowing the horn, Rizzo came out of the house in his work suit jumper with the wife and her other family members standing at the doorway pleading that Victoria stop beeping the horn and being disruptive.

Victoria got out of the car and said, "I didn't have any issue with you until this very moment. You served the divorce papers; Rizzo signed them, and we all had dinner and a conversation about it. So, at this time of night, you're here, what is the problem?" The response that Rizzo gave Victoria blew her away. It was as if he fired another explosive bomb of deception when he told her that he needed to get some jumper cables and he knew that at that time of night his wife would have his old jumper cables, and so he stopped to get them from their house.

Victoria looked at Rizzo and then she looked at his wife, and she became even more enraged. He walked closer trying to console her while the wife just watched, because she had already said that she was used to this type of behavior from him. In that moment Victoria regained her dignity and slapped Rizzo in the face and told him that they were done. She went home she packed up all of his belongings and poured bleach on them and threw them in the trash. However, he followed behind her apologizing so that he can regain her trust. But she had finally learned her lesson in spite of the fact that this man was the father of her children. In Victoria's mind, this relationship was dead. She had been through so much with men who was only seeking to be manipulative.

But she did not care anymore. In fact, within the next few days Victoria started to find a new place to live. She became really withdrawn and could barely eat. She took time off from her job because she had felt that she had put her everything into someone and she lost it all. It was a real lesson for her, and the lesson was to never put your all into anyone because when they walk away you won't have anything left, especially if it's the wrong person. During this time Victoria leaned heavily on her father who came to her aid. He was very consoling and helpful with the boys because there were days that she could not eat or sleep. She relied on her father, and she used that time to just love on her sons. This gave her the strength she needed to be able to move on.

Victoria moved on and never looked back. She moved out of her home immediately, going into a hotel for two weeks while she was waiting for a place to live and an apartment to come through. The point of it all is that in life sometimes you have to do what you have to do until you are able to do what you want to do. You also need to do what you need to do in order to ensure that you have the mental strength and capacity to live in your truth… period. She learned that you have to live life in a way that is free of anxiety rather than one that is filled with deception, deceit, and betrayal. You have to know when to hold on and when to let someone go. And that is exactly what Victoria did at that moment. She just let go.

Shots were once again be fired in Victoria's life, but she overcame the agony and rebuilt her life through the recovery of spiritual gems and truths, through strong relationships with family and friends that were there to support her during a very dismal time in her life. In a time where things seemed bleak and there was no hope, the only saving grace was the joy that she felt when she saw her children's faces. As a parent she learned that she had to be vulnerable, but she had to show strength and show her kids that she was strong and never allowed them to see someone that is supposed to love them, mistreat them. She had vowed that she would never subject her kids to the trauma that she had experienced.

She experienced situations where she had seen someone get beat against a radiator or someone beaten by a loved one and receive a black eye from their mate. Victoria knew that the love that she had for her sons was every bit unconditional and that she owed them everything. It was her responsibility and her duty to be the best example of what a woman is supposed to be. And that first and foremost, she had to respect herself enough to never allow someone to cause her emotional distress to the detriment of her children.

Lessons Learned: Life and love go hand in hand, and one must navigate with their eyes wide open. People will show you who they are, so believe the actions. The hardest thing to do is to walk away from a toxic situation, but staying is like drinking poison and expecting someone to die. So, make the hard decisions and know when to go.

CHAPTER 15

Children Are Not Stray Bullets

No doubt Victoria knew that by her leaving her children's father, it was going to be a battle of a lifetime. She knew that she would not endure the deception and betrayal, but that her children would not be left uncared for or treated like stray bullets being left out to land wherever. In fact, Victoria had already decided that there would be no regrets in her decision to have her children with their father Rizzo. Victoria had already accepted the responsibility and strength it was going to take to raise her children on her own. Her four young men became her motivation in life and the reason why every decision she made going forward was made with them in mind. Although one of her sons had a father that was involved and the other three were without Rizzo, she was committed to motherhood and vowed to herself that no man would ever become more important than her children. The lesson for her was understanding that each parent's commitment could look very different. Meaning that although she did not grow up with her parents in the home, her mother made a commitment to doing what was best for Victoria.

Although Rizzo immediately made a decision in response to the hurt that he felt. As a result of Victoria's decision, there was no doubt that he didn't love Victoria, because he did. But it was obvious that he wanted to have his cake and eat it too. Victoria was never going to allow his continued deception and disrespect for her as a woman, but she needed to forgive herself. In essence, Victoria needed to extend herself the grace to become the best woman and mother she could become without allowing a man to cast doubts on her worthiness. It was no longer realistic for her to believe that he would give her loyalty and love. Instead, he stole the very essence of her trust by seeking his own pleasures for his own selfish reasons. Victoria had already gotten to the point where she knew she had to have a firm stand on her decision to do what was best for her sons.

However, Rizzo could not accept this. He told Victoria that she was responsible for destroying their family and therefore he could not be in a relationship with her or his sons. For Victoria, hearing these words felt like being shot in the face! It was hoped at this point that the separation and severance of their relationship would be seamless, but it did not turn out that way at all. In fact, it was the exact opposite.

Rizzo had begun stalking Victoria, shortly after their breakup. She moved and stayed in a hotel for almost three weeks. She had to get a two-bedroom hotel room with a kitchen unit so she could prepare meals, chill with her kids, and commute daily to and from work. It was also convenient for school for drop off and pick up. The amount of her stay cost a small fortune. Fortunately, Victoria was starting to thrive in her career and had begun developing a plan to start a side hustle in network marketing in order to generate another source of income.

The lesson she learned was to never depend on a man to take care of everything for you and that if you can't afford to take care of it yourself, to always have a back-up plan. By this time, she had become established in her career, but felt that she was missing out on fun, so she contacted an associate to hang out with the one she called "the Snake". However, before Victoria could even consider going out and enjoying her mid-twenties lifestyle, a harsh reality became her life for the next few years.

After the boy's father was out of the picture, her son started to act out as a result of the separation. The reality was that kids can only express their emotions in a limited capacity but their behavior speaks volumes. At this time her youngest son was only two years old and for the life of her she could not understand how obsessed her son was with pork and beans, especially since she rarely cooked hot dogs and beans at home. Nonetheless, her son, Nico had a fit and showed out in his classroom at the daycare. Niko was the cutest, smallest little boy with the prettiest hair, but with an attitude that was very hard to bear. So, when Victoria received the call from the school, she had no idea that they were going to inform her that her two-year-old son had fallen out onto the floor in a full-blown tantrum, to the point that when he hit the floor his front tooth came flying out of his mouth.

Victoria was devastated and confused with her emotions running wild. She had no clue as to how he could be so upset that he would have a tantrum and then lose a tooth over some food. Needless to say, this was truly a moment of clarity, that this was just the beginning of what lay ahead. Once the drama started, the days started running together. But she knew she had to be resilient in the midst of adversity. She had to be an advocate for her sons that dealt with mental challenges. Although she was not legally married to Rizzo the devastation of his absence hit her children hard. It was as if they had literally been shot by stray bullets and left for dead by their father.

There would be multiple calls throughout the years when Victoria would have to leave in the midst of a meeting to tend to a family emergency at the school. In one scenario, her son turned a classroom upside down throwing everything around and in a rage; then hits the principal who's trying to calm him down, by accident. There were moments where Victoria seemed to be gasping for air because in her mind, physically abusing her children was not an option. Although she disciplined her sons, she had never herself been beaten with a belt, or a stick, or any other things that all of the older people said that she needed to hit her kids with.

In fact, Victoria was a champion for her sons, and she knew that it had to be something wrong with them for them to act out in the manner that they did. So, contrary to popular opinion, and having been a recipient of emotional support and counseling that sustained her mental health, she sought to find out how to ensure that her children could receive the emotional and mental support they needed.

Upon speaking with the school, the challenge that she faced was that she was not a welfare recipient and therefore the community programs were not available to her because she was employed and had built a career. The unfortunate reality of this situation was that there was a system that only provided services if your child was a statistic in the juvenile court system. This was the most absurd thing she ever had to go through.

By this time her youngest son had now become seven years old, and the older brothers had been relocated to different schools. Victoria also searched for places that offered assistance and yet again, she found none. Her health insurance at the time didn't initially cover mental health, as her son was diagnosed with having ADHD and had years of documented occurances of disturbance.

Victoria knew that she needed to take matters into her own hands, and therefore she started reaching out to community groups outside of the network. She started consulting with different school jurisdictions and after almost two years, she saw a commercial about how to hire an advocate attorney for children with special needs, which included attention deficit disorder, also known as ADD. This was a very critical moment for Victoria and no doubt a pivot that would change the dynamic of her child's future. She knew that by this time next year she would have been able to have her children evaluated and assigned an advocate attorney that would be proactive in how she handled her dealings with the school system. Her primary goal was to ensure that her children were provided with the necessary tools to help improve their mental and emotional stability. Within weeks, she built a rapport with her advisor who was working on developing a case by obtaining background information of her family as well as that of Rizzo's.

In this moment, Victoria felt empowered. She knew that by being an advocate for her own children, she was the voice that they needed when they couldn't be a voice for themselves. Whenever she needed to, she would sound the alarm that showed she definitely was not playing when it came to saving the lives of her sons. During the course of her journey, it was enlightening to understand the dynamics of behaviors that were inherited versus learned behavior, and the impacts this society has on young children of color.

All of the things that she had learned growing up, including the Christian family values that she was taught, she would try to instill within her sons. It sometimes became surreal as the barriers, the boundaries, the discipline, and the nurturing became key elements to her children's success.

No doubt, the lesson Victoria learned was that the Bible held the key to many things, if not everything that she had to endure as a parent. Although it may not have been specific in dealing with the exact nature of the situation, it was very clear that the principles set the guidance. Although it was not easy, she used it to mold, develop, and groom her sons to be respectable and very intelligent young men.

During this period of time, Victoria would spend at least one day a week either visiting the school speaking to the principals or dealing with a behavior issue with at least two of her sons. The challenge was ensuring that the attention given to bad behavior was given in a way that they would not feel left out or excluded.

Victoria's best efforts to make that happen were unfortunately not well received. In the long run, she learned that things can never be fully balanced because there's always a situation where a person or something that's going to tilt the scales. She had become a very involved mother as a parent team committee member for the schools. She was also a team mom for the community involvement programs for her children. She was the cool mom that all of her sons' friends loved to be around because she did so many things with them. She enjoyed sports and she made the children always feel included.

The irony of it all is that as well as things seemed to be put together, it seemed that society emphasized and encouraged bad behavior as well as being on welfare. And the impact that this has on children whose parents have to work to provide for them a comfortable lifestyle nine times out of ten was challenging. Yet, those that are the most poverty stricken and receive public assistance are often the children that are walking around with the latest name brand-named shoes but not the other things that they need to succeed in life.

Victoria learned that what that does is gives the impression that the household that's being given public assistance has a false sense of wealth. Whereas the household with the children whose parents work, that have nice things but not be materialistic, get to see that you have to earn them. Working parents try to teach their children that some things aren't just given because there are other real expenses such as maintaining a mortgage, paying a car note or car insurance, and paying unsubsidized utility bills. She learned that what this does for children who are just given things is that it creates a longing for more, quickly, without actually working for it.

So, what that did for Victoria was it made her want to have to work more to instill in her sons that although people have these nice things you have to have a sense of balance within yourself and to be realistic about what you can and cannot afford. Many of the people that were walking around looking like a billboard advertisement for whatever high end fashion designer that was available could also be broke, and they had no cash in their bank accounts. They did not understand what it was to pay for food because the food was given to them for free essentially because they were being purchased with food stamps.

A hard lesson that her kids had to learn as they became young men was to realize the importance of hard work and not trying to take shortcuts that would result in outcomes that was not in their best interest. She had often told them nothing in life is free. You have to earn what you want, and hard work is what's going to get you those things. She taught them that you have to be strategic in your thinking and that you cannot be a follower or get involved in any type of scam or crime without expecting some type of consequences.

And the crazy thing was Victoria always told her children because you are different you are always gonna stand out. The fact that your parents did not have to rely on the welfare system is gonna also be a reason why you will be different and held more accountable for your actions. In the long run, if you get involved with anything that's illegal, you will pay.

Well, you're always going to have some children that will listen, and then you have those that will test the waters. Victoria had to endure those moments where her children tested the waters in and out of the juvenile judicial system from the age of sixteen. Her two middle kids started getting in trouble for things that were so minute, like hanging out past dark or breaking a curfew past midnight, which meant that you were leaving the house seeking out trouble and now you're gonna be punished for it.

Unfortunately, in the District of Columbia, a violation of curfew is a reflection of neglect by the parents, and so if you want to be a good parent and your children secretly leave out the house, you're held accountable even if you were asleep. Or you are responsible if someone gave them a phone, you're receiving a stolen property unbeknownst to you, but they don't know because they are getting too caught up in doing what their friends are doing and they're not used to a life of crime or anything, but the consequences are still grave for them.

As time went on her sons became incarcerated because they were just curious. Victoria really felt she had lost. The lesson for her was a hard one to accept, especially because she had done everything in her power to help them. The hardest thing that a parent can do is to be worried about a child that is incarcerated in prison because you really have no clue of what's going on and what's happening to them. The agony of worry and fear is so overwhelming, especially when you have to go weeks or months without hearing from your child wondering if they are dead or alive.

Think about it like this. If your child is killed on the street you're gonna grieve, but you're gonna feel a small sense of comfort knowing that you can go to their burial site and visit their grave as opposed to if your child is in prison and they're on lockdown and they can't see you, they can't call you, they may not even be able to write you. In those moments Victoria felt defeated because unlike all the time she had been a parent, she was her children's advocate. But during this time when her son was incarcerated, her advocating to the warden, only made things worse, so she couldn't do anything but rely on God and pray and that's what she did.

And that is the point where she really realized that consequences can be far greater than imagined. Consequences of people's choices don't just impact the children, but they impact their parents and as a single mother it was so hard. Not to mention the fact that now her children are starting to have children. In fact, there was an instance where her son had recently become incarcerated, and he ask her to go to a doctor's appointment to meet the young lady that was not his girlfriend but that he had been dealing with so that his mom could be there when he couldn't. In essence what he asked her to do was to be there for the birth of his child, especially since he had been sentenced and he knew that he wasn't going to be there.

And his mom did just that. In fact, on the day that her grandchild was born, Victoria was out of town and had to take a flight back so that she could be there upon the arrival of her grandchild being born into this world. So, the point of it all is that although Victoria was left with a tremendous responsibility, and it was burdensome for her, it never changed the fact that she wanted to be the best for her children.

To receive the blessings of bearing children made her feel more like a woman and she deeply embraced motherhood. She had not realized what she was missing out on until she was actually pregnant and had her children. Before then she had not wanted any kids, and so how could you miss what you never had. This was the thought that came to her when she was pregnant with her first child. She realized that in that moment she had been very selfish and so she had long made amends to ensure that she would do everything she could to raise her kids to the best of her ability in spite of the fact that she herself had been broken and had gone without. She just made a point to do better than what her parents did and ensured that through the years she restored any relationship that she didn't have with her parents to make sure that they had it with them as grandparents.

For Victoria, life was about making choices. So, she made a decision to pour into her children and did all that she could for her family even in the most difficult situations all the while building her career, which was also very challenging. In the next chapter we will meet the career woman -- Miss Victoria.

Lessons Learned – Nothing in life is given or received without an impact. Success is not measured by what you have, but plan for success and prepare for challenges as failure is on the road that leads to understanding and winning in the game of life.

CHAPTER 16

Fully Loaded... Guns Blazing

"Excuse me...how can I help you, because if you're looking for the hair salon, then it's located on the 2nd floor", was the question that Victoria was asked by the black receptionist who appeared to be in her early twenties. Victoria responded, "This is the 6th?"

After leaving her full-time job to do temp work, she already had one child and was 4 months pregnant with her second son. Now, although Victoria was professionally dressed in her black, slim fit, Ann Taylor suit and her black heels, she was wearing a platinum blonde full weave, which could have caused the confusion with the receptionist. She was at the Chief Executive Office for a three-week assignment as an Accounts Payable Technician. But Victoria didn't take offense and just simply smiled and respectfully asked for Mrs. Frost, the Manager. Suddenly, the receptionist had a look of embarrassment on her face and in that moment, Victoria immediately leaned over to her and said "girl it's the hair, and it's okay because next week it will be a different color" ... and they both laughed. Now that was the first of the many looks that she would receive from the older black women, except for the one who was the Payroll Manager and believed in zodiac signs.

Mrs. Harris, who had also been near the receptionist's desk on the first day, was impressed by Victoria's response. A few days later, Victoria was formally introduced to Mrs. Harris, who immediately asked Victoria when her birthday was, and when she responded that she was born in the same month as she was, Mrs. Harris shouted…" I knew it…and don't you worry honey about these people, just do your job, because I've been here for 30 years, and I've seen them come and I've seen them go. But you have what it takes to really grow and excel if you keep a sense of humor, do your job and let your work speak for itself. Believe me…you'll see them come and go, too." Victoria then responded in her true optimist voice…saying "thank you and this has been the story of my life, so I'm ready, because I'm not just here for me, I'm here to build a career for my family and all that I can do is be authentically me."

Victoria was one that definitely hit the ground running. She came in with guns blazing to showcase her skills that well exceeded expectations. And just like that, Victoria was invested, and she didn't realize just how much of an impact that Mrs. Harris had on the decision of who would stay and who would go, as a result of her years of stellar performance and great achievement in balancing payrolls for more than 1800 employees with a payroll staff of only two people. But Victoria would soon realize that first impressions mattered and that relationships opened the pathway to her success.

During those days Victoria was in her early twenties. She walked in already knowing fully what to expect because her grandparents and her aunt and uncle prepared her and instilled in her the importance of being confident. No doubt she was reassured of her skills and had a willingness to work. She was customer service oriented, and she was a natural born leader. Victoria already had the innate skills to win, and she was winning when everyone was expecting her to lose. Within those three weeks Victoria showcased her skills. She was consistent and worked independently.

She listened, she learned, she observed, and she made sure that she connected with the key players that were the decision makers. Having been amongst other seasoned women that were black, they were able to recognize talent at an executive level. She worked tirelessly through the end of the fiscal year and when the deputy CFO and the chief of staff became aware of her knowledge and skills as well as the energy that she bought to the team, he knew that they needed to keep her, so she was given an extension for another three months.

She certainly had not expected to transition so quickly and was honestly looking forward to being in a temporary role so that she could maintain her family life and be home. Anyway, she was so insightful for her age and could look at where she needed to be and make the decisions with foresight and the vision to implement them. From the first appearance, her skills spoke volumes. She was great at executing in a way that led to sustainability. At this time, she remembered what she had learned from her aunt, who was the human resources manager at a private firm. She was taught to keep working, and keep your business to yourself, because no one needs to know that you're pregnant, and Victoria did just that.

By the end of the calendar year, she was offered a job opportunity with the team. This allowed her to gain employment full-time, less than a week before the expected delivery date of her twins. By now she had obviously become pregnant and was fully showing. Immediately upon being hired, she went out on maternity leave, but she had impressed them all so much that they were so supportive of her leave that when they knew that she didn't have enough hours, they worked to assist her with other duties so that she could essentially telework and get paid.

However, during the transition of management she would often have to deal with the onslaught of naysayers. And yet, the most surprising thing was that it was always the black woman. In fact, a black woman had an issue with her hair, or told her that she needed to make sure she always kept a blazer on the back of her chair, or that she could not get a promotion because she wasn't ready to be among the wolves and didn't want her to be cast out like a stone.

They didn't want to give her the promotion because they were protecting her? Go figure. Yet, the very thing that they thought they were protecting her from was the very thing that many of the executives embraced. Her skills were something that was respected by the leaders regardless of their race or gender.

There was a time that Victoria was told within the five years of her being in her position, that her numbers were all that the Director wanted to see. It became so crazy that her manager had become furious. She would give the praise to Victoria that she was once given because the Director told her "Any numbers that come from the finance team is like coming from a black hole, so unless it comes from Victoria, I don't want to see them." So, since this was stated in the executive meeting that both Victoria and her Supervisor attended, the Supervisor became very spiteful.

It was as if she was jealous of this young aspiring professional at every turn. Victoria was just looking to excel, and she had never shaded anyone. In fact, she befriended her manager and was always respectful to her, but that didn't matter. It had gotten so bad that once her manager completed her evaluation stating that she didn't come to visit her enough in her office. What was interesting about this scenario is that Victoria never felt intimidated by anyone at any level or at any age, so upon reading her evaluation she spoke up for herself. She was always taught to speak about how she felt and so she did. She informed her supervisor that she did not agree with what she had written about her and that what she stated was purely personal and did not have anything to do with her work.

In addition, Victoria had always loved to write as it was very therapeutic for her. So, it was an easy transition to write emails to send notifications because she was familiar with those things, and she did this all the time when she was young. She wrote poems, she wrote letters to her friend that moved away who had been like a sister to her. And so, when it came to work, she felt that she had transferable skills. That also became a key factor in her life because Victoria documented every time she submitted any request, any reports and she always sent updates to her manager. This became a trademark of Victoria throughout her career.

These skills were especially reinforced when she joined a professional organization and became the transcriber of what was being dictated by the committee when she would sit in on the meetings. She literally took notes for the members. Those sessions would be about strategic and organizational development, which would be the key to her professional development. The jewels that she learned from the professional black executive women that were in the company became very impactful. She learned from her new supervisor and the executive leaders of the company who embraced her talent. So having had those innate skills, she always wanted to learn more so it would stand to reason that she absorbed the information while taking notes.

Those moments were also transformative because when she would present her case to the executives about how she was being treated unfairly for personal reasons, she could then show her work that was well-documented, and they had her back. They realized that she was not in a position to win and that it was their responsibility as managers and supervisors as the executive leadership team that they had to strategically move her to a better position. What they did was to have all of the senior executive team take a 360-personality assessment. They would then develop coaching based on the responses. However, because the Director provided the update that they were preparing and executing the budget, and the Director stated that Victoria year end projection and financial analysis reports were the only ones with accurate numbers, Victoria was included in the 360-assessment opportunity, making her the youngest person included in the executive coaching series.

When the results came back indeed it was mind blowing! Victoria was the perfect balance with her results identifying her as equally dominant and conscientious as a leader in all aspects of her personality assessment. To further understand the meaning of the assessment, the conscientious personality types have the tendency to be more organized, responsible, goal oriented, hard- working and follow the rules of society. In comparison, a dominant personality type is someone that has the tendency to be dominant in the sense that they are very confident and assertive, because they know what they want.

However, Victoria's supervisor, on the other hand, scored in the 10% percentile for being a conscientious person and almost 90% percentile for a domineering personality type. Well, this was mind blowing not to just the senior executive team, but to her supervisor as well. At that moment, the team realized that her supervisor truly didn't know how to supervise Victoria and needed to make a major personality transformation.

Upon the discovery of this information, the immediate supervisor requested to have a meeting with Victoria. The supervisor stated to her, "I do not know how to manage you. Go figure, you are twenty-four years old, and I am forty." This was a much-needed conversation because this was also a pivotal point in their communication with each other and would ultimately be the dynamic that changed their interaction on a professional and personal level. The order went forward to reassign Victoria to another division. This move also allowed her to flourish in her professional career and take it to another level.

In addition, Victoria loved network marketing ventures and at the time was in the business of selling Cutco knives and prepaid legal services, which were allowing those in the minority to gain access to an attorney in the event of racial profiling or any legal matter where they need to have representation at a price that was affordable, as they would ultimately always be retained. Well, that idea and that business venture was very intriguing to Victoria's supervisor, as they had gotten to the point where they could have a conversation that was just not based on the work itself in the office. This allowed Victoria to be able to be comfortable with expressing her endeavors that were occurring outside of the office during lunch or breaks or times that they were interacting with each other since they were no longer were in a supervisor and subordinate arrangement.

And it proved to be very beneficial for the both of them because the supervisor ultimately joined the network marketing business which therefore allowed for promotional growth for Victoria to move into a level of management that resulted in a situation where both she and the former supervisor traveled to various locations to present on the product that they were selling.

Lessons Learned: No doubt the lesson here was stand firm, know your worth and have those critical conversations, even if it means that you have to be uncomfortable in an environment that ultimately will result in you being comfortable, but only if you stand up for yourself in the most professional and respectable manner. In addition, Victoria learned the importance of being able to be fearless yet humble, tactful and always maintaining grace when dealing with people regardless of age, gender or race.

CHAPTER 17

A Shot at Success

Now in the beginning, it was mentioned how Victoria grew up with her grandparents and she learned a lot of insights that would be very helpful in the development and enhancement of Victoria's career. It is also important to speak about the significance regarding who your parents were and how it also hindered Victoria from going to a level of elevation that she wanted and ultimately attained on her own. But she had not yet arrived financially.

Throughout the years she was always challenged with the concern of her appearance and particularly her hair color. So, Victoria learned that sometimes you have to take a step back in order to reposition yourself, then go back up to the level where you want to be. In this particular instance when she was referenced to by her hair color, she changed it. Victoria realized that it was back in the early 2000's and they were not ready to accept the generation of millennials with the various hair colors, and multi-level clothing, and creative weaves for the black women in the work environment.

There was another situation where she got turned down for a promotion that she was told she was guaranteed to get. However, when Victoria did not get the promotion, she remained calm and did not allow the upset of others who felt that she deserved it, to change her demeanor, or even how she interacted with her supervisor. This was a real mindset change for Victoria. In fact, Victoria's mindset was one of: what she didn't gain in financial wealth she would ensure that she gained in a wealth of knowledge, and she kept this mindset throughout her career.

By this time, it was the late 2000's and Victoria was now pregnant with her fourth son. There was a period of five years since the birth of her previous son, and she had various sprints where she had small wins where she helped change the culture of the organization by her recommendations.

Victoria was wise beyond her years as it related to being able to think outside of the box, from developing innovative methods to streamlining processes for improvement. As a result, a developmental transition plan was created that would allow Victoria to shadow the administrator for six months in order for her to become fully immersed and prepared for the job ahead as a department administrator. However, unbeknownst to the other administrators, towards the end of the year Victoria could no longer hide the fact that she was pregnant yet again. It was the Fall fiscal year 2006, and Victoria attended the organization wide budget kickoff meeting. She had already applied for the position of administrator because the position would be vacated within a month. She was selected to take over that role.

However, once she was observed to be pregnant, that very next week she was notified that the position had been canceled and her offer rescinded. This was very disappointing to Victoria, but she was still very young and was fully aware that she was being discriminated against for being pregnant but was not able to prove what was happening. There is no doubt that all women can now appreciate the Pregnancy Act of 2014 which allows for women to not be discriminated against for being pregnant. In addition, it allows for women to be given equal opportunity for job employment and the ability to have the nursing stations and other comfort amenities at work along with additional time off as needed to ensure that they take off and for the care of their children.

As Victoria reflected on the fact that if the opportunity had been given to her back then, she would be much further along in her career. Although she may not be where she wants to be in life, in terms of her happiness with her family and her kids, she ultimately wanted to be in a position that allowed her to become a wife that was focused on family first and no longer that of her career.

You would have thought that all of this would have broken Victoria, but it didn't. Not getting that position made her realize her worth even more, and she needed to develop her exit plan. She realized that she could no longer stay in a place where trust was broken and the discrimination was so blatant. However, she knew she still needed to represent herself in the most professional manner and to never allow her demeanor and her work ethics to ever slack.

Once again, she made a decision to be conscious about her next move, and that meant obtaining additional education to be more prepared to achieve her goal. This "knowledge gaining" strategy allowed Victoria to become credentialed as a Microsoft certified user for all of the systems that included Word, Excel, Access and PowerPoint. Having this formalized training led to her becoming a Subject Matter Expert. In addition, Victoria allowed this experience to motivate her to do more as it related to literacy and networking. But this time internally within her organization and not just outside. During this time, Victoria also developed relationships with external stakeholders and her work did not go unnoticed. She was already thinking strategically about her next move after the delivery of her baby upon returning to work. She had already been offered another position that would still maintain that she would be working at the same building.

And the beauty of it all was that Victoria still learned to maintain relationships with those that made the promises even though they did not keep them; or those that discriminated against her because of her age or because of the fact that she was pregnant. Despite all of those issues, Victoria still remained authentic and never looked down on anyone. She never held anything against anyone, and she remained focused on being the best that she could be. Most of all she always worked on being a humble servant leader.

Victoria recognized early in life that she cannot be responsible for the actions of others and that she could only be responsible for herself. She also realized that every day she had to make a conscious decision to not to hold grudges despite all adversities because she also accepted the fact that no one was perfect. This important lesson was instilled in her very early about having integrity, understanding, compassion, and being ethical. To always extend grace, even to those that may not deserve it, was also key. With that type of mindset and Victoria's determination to become the master of her own success, helped her embrace the transition to a new role that did not give her a financial gain but allowed her the opportunity to thrive in an environment where she could be self-sufficient.

Another major accomplishment that Victoria had was the fact that every system that she selected to study would also be the very system that she would get an opportunity to develop, implement and train the more than 900 employees that previously used a paper timesheet. The employees gained new insights from Victoria's training and learned how to utilize a computer for the first time in their lives. She also had the opportunity to train people on how to own their paychecks by assuring that they learned how to enter their pay through a software system. This was an amazing opportunity because this was something that she had never done at that magnitude. Victoria was the one that trained all of those people and coordinated the training with the assistance of her team within the human resources division.

This was a major milestone for Victoria, and after all she had been through, she still remained humble. She knew that the commitment and compassion that she showed, and the wealth of knowledge that she had gained at this point in her life would eventually pay off. And, that the notoriety of being a subject matter expert and her work ethics, her drive, her motivation, her consistency, her commitment would soon impact her income.

Victoria often thought of the many people that needed to understand that being a leader was more than just the title you have but rather it was more about how you treated people. She also believed that it had a lot to do with how you developed relationships and how you communicate with people. So, by this time in Victoria's life, the role of Vice President of Operations also allowed for her to take on more highly trusted roles.

This was a big deal for Victoria because in addition to all of those duties, she still maintained the ability to manage and build the budget for her department, the office of the Director, and that of the Chief of Staff. At this point in Victoria's career, she had truly developed a reputation of one that gets the job done as well as one that has always exuded excellent customer service to every person that she ever dealt with regardless of their race, classification or where they worked.

Victoria would always tell people that she was a geek and loved a challenge. She was able to overcome in all aspects of her personal life and now she was victorious in her professional life. The very purpose of her work was to show her sons that consistency and commitment can lead to success and so much more. It was important for her to help them understand that to attain a level of happiness and comfortability in your life can be achieved by hard work. No doubt, it was this mindset that would carry on throughout her professional journey to her vision of successfully implementing all these programs while maintaining a level of excellence for the company.

In 2010, the very company that she left in finance had conducted an audit that identified that the organization was non-compliant with federal regulations as it related to contract compliance. So, when this bad news came, they needed to have a dedicated expert to assess the issue of non-compliance and develop a long- and short-term plan for a process improvement. In addition to transitioning information to an electronic process that currently was a ninety-nine percent manual paper process. They immediately identified Victoria as the first person to be up for the challenge. Upon being told this news, Victoria was ecstatic and willing to help, but she knew that she needed to gain a financial increase.

She learned at this point the importance of knowing how to negotiate and ask for what you want, realizing they could never pay her what she was truly worth. By this time Victoria had been in her career for well over fifteen years, which exceeded her initial plan, which was to "be in an organization for no more than fifteen years, before becoming a full-time entrepreneur". But in reality, it was not that she didn't plan well, she would become a person that had completed all her goals.

Now that the job was no longer fulfilling, she needed to move on to something else because she had established a brand and a legacy in all of her previous roles. Having become a person that learned from her experiences and how to reflect and make better decisions, she continued to go forward realizing her worth. Yet again, she knew that they needed her and so this was her opportunity to fulfill her dream and ask that her salary be set over the $100,000 mark. It was no surprise that although she had not yet completed her full degree program, she did have numerous certifications and trainings. Because she was a continuous learner, her salary increase request was granted.

This was a game changer for Victoria, and it ignited in her the idea that she needed to make sure that she could be a coach to people who may not have been as discerning as she was or afforded the opportunities she had. She could teach them how they could deal with similar situations and circumstances. It made her reflect that she wanted to be a person that poured into others just as she herself had always been like a sponge where she would learn and absorb from others. Similarly, she could be rung out like a sponge for others and be poured back out into them.

During the next 10 years Victoria would deal with assessing the non-compliance issues. She had the pleasure of creating, developing, implementing, and executing a business within a business. She was given full reign over how she created her division. All the years of her experience and budget and human resources in compliance were coming full circle. She knew how to write and prepare her budget request and submit her budget formulation plan. She also wrote and researched her positions based on her ability to conduct studies which included benchmarks from other similar organizations within the United States of America. She collaborated amongst other groups and peers within the federal government that resulted in stakeholders from Japan wanting to meet with Victoria and her organization, so that they could gain insights from her on how she managed contractor compliance and wages.

She read compliance principles and the personnel manuals often to assure that she was being kept abreast of all the latest information that would be impactful when she hired consulting firms to assist with the workload. She returned to higher learning and obtained her degree and other accreditations. This would ultimately transition to building capacity for long-term employment on a permanent basis. She developed and wrote standard operating procedures and created workflow charts to ensure that the process of understanding was user-friendly for all involved.

Victoria thrived in this moment of success just like she hoped she would. Her clarity and her conduct allowed her to become the master of her own success as a servant leader. The payoff was greater than any amount that was on her paycheck. Why? Because some things are worth more than the paper that she was being paid with. It was the fact that her ideas became a reality that eventually resulted in the sustainability of a human capital infrastructure that afforded people the opportunity to have employment in an environment where pay harmonization was very dismal. This was an opportunity for Victoria to be of service to those that may not even know the value for them, but it was priceless to her. Priceless because all she ever wanted was to be a voice to those that needed to be heard as she had known long before now, what her purpose and mission was in life, and that was to serve people to give genuinely from the heart all that she had whether it was of her time, money, or energy. To be a giver was the foundation of her own happiness.

But like anything else, Victoria was leery that at some point someone or something was going to attempt to try to shoot down the legacy of success that she had built. Although she hired people, fired people, built up and encouraged people, motivated people, and was kind to everyone… her worse night-mares became a reality.

She would have never expected that one of her very few friends in her small circle would be the very person that would try to assassinate her credibility and threaten her livelihood because she had changed her life and accepted God.

Lessons Learned: A person that fails to plan will always plan to fail. However, having a plan is the blueprint to winning, as long as one continues to adjust and modify the course to see the plan to its end.

CHAPTER 18

The Bullet of Betrayal

I t's hard to believe that the very people you chose to associate with a very extended period of time could perpetrate their loyalty, betray you, and try to assassinate you. Victoria was at the height of her career and was always optimistic. She honestly reflected on her success realizing that it's gonna always come with envy and jealousy. However, this was nothing new to Victoria because she had always experienced unforeseen occurrences and knew that there are things in life it's almost always going to happen.

Whether it was dealing with a court case for her sons, or having issues amongst individuals in the workplace, Victoria never thought about the fact that the very person whom she had deep connections with would betray her, especially those who were in a position to help when others had tried to hurt her. So, when this "supposed" friend would refer to Victoria as "the CEO of her organization", due to her success in the workplace, this really showed how much of a "Snake" she was. Now Victoria realized that she was a very intentional Snake that longed to be in the position that Victoria held, and purposefully did things to prove it. As Victoria reflected on this whole scenario and the deliberate acts of this individual, she thought about the numerous occasions this snake appeared to help. But on a particular occasion when Victoria tried to help her in a way that literally would change this person's life, only for her to stab her in the back, talk bad about her family, and how Victoria was jealous of two people whom the Snake had only met a few months before. This was compounded by the fact that Victoria considered this person as a friend coached and hired her in order for her to become employed at her organization.

The interesting thing about this whole situation is that in previous years, Victoria had given her authority to take over Victoria's apartment, because Victoria had purchased a condo. Victoria should have known better because this same Snake actually left unpaid rent and utility bills in Victoria's name that was never brought to her attention until she filed for bankruptcy and a week before her discharge date her attorney informed her of these bills that were now being presented to the court for payment. Upon Victoria finding out this information, she immediately contacted the Snake and inquired about the outstanding rental, bills, and court costs that totaled more than $10,000. Being the optimist that Victoria was, and the person who was always looking to resolve a situation, she simply told her to just pay the adjustment fee of $100 so that she could amend her bankruptcy and the issue would have been settled. The Snake agreed however the next day when the payment was supposed to be made to Victoria, she did not answer the phone or answer the door when Victoria went to her house even though she was in the house when Victoria came to the door stating, "I'm just not giving it to you because I don't think I should".

Needless to say, at this point Victoria was taken aback because she had always prided herself on the fact that everyone that was in association with her knew that she did not play about her family, her money, or her livelihood Therefore, Victoria felt that in this moment this Snake should have undoubtedly been willing to pay for the adjustment to the bankruptcy that Victoria was filing because she was the one who created the charges and expenses.

At this point, Victoria felt betrayed by this fake friend that was supposed to have her best interest at heart, solely based on principle. Instead, she was only looking for personal gain because she was broke and took the opportunity to go against Victoria and take advantage of her. As a result, Victoria acknowledged and accepted her for who she was at that time because she was older than Victoria, but she was very young minded. Victoria made a decision to walk away from that situation for years despite the fact that they had witnessed the birth of each other 's children. They often would go out to clubs together. Regardless of their supposed sister-friend experiences together, they were not on the same level when it came to business.

Now, about ten years would go by before they would even see each other again. And their supposed friendship was reconciled largely due to the fact that they didn't have the same circle of friends and therefore there was no negativity discussed. In victorious fashion, Victoria did not gossip, so on the few occasions when someone that may have known of the both of them would ask about how they were doing, Victoria response would always be I haven't heard from her but I'm sure she's well. Eventually Victoria did see her at a gas station, and she was pregnant. They reconnected because it appeared that the Snake was apologetic for not being responsible and paying Victoria the money, she owed her. So Victoria accepted her apology and they reconciled because Victoria had always been a very forgiving person. Although the nature of their interactions had changed, and they were no longer as close as they had been before, they became associates.

During this time in Victoria's life, she was transitioning yet from another relationship and was living single, so she would go out to the clubs occasionally, but not as often as the Snake, since it remained a known fact that lifestyle was the young lady's life and that's what she continued to do for years, so they would occasionally go out. But that was the extent of their reconciled friendship. It never was a discussion of business and Victoria did not stay around long enough or attend events at her home. Yet again there was a situation where the young lady needed a home due to living in poor conditions. Ironically, Victoria had just vacated a rental home property because one of her sons had become irate and addicted to drugs, and Victoria no longer wanted to live there since he refused to move and was just turning eighteen. Victoria still was willing to help people because that's who she was, and she didn't know how to be anything other than authentically herself. Victoria learned the lesson from the last time and so Victoria knew she needed to make sure that she put these things in writing. When you realize who people are you, have to accept them for who they are. Sure enough, lo and behold, this Snake, yet again, did not pay for the security deposit initially which was agreed upon. However, Victoria said "Well, if you leave then you'll just pay me then." Well, that didn't happen considering the young lady left the house again with the bills unpaid.

Yet again, Victoria was dealing with situations and struggles with her kids that required her to relocate without her now grown sons. She had to be strategic about her next move and now had to make a decision to change her life personally, and no longer live a life of a single woman. This would mean that the next realm of her adulthood, in becoming a woman, she would become a wife. What that meant was that the principles that Victoria had always instilled in her kids, one being: that a setback is a setup for a comeback. This was still very much something that she also lived by. So, she decided to move into an apartment and sublease the home that she lived in previously. This time, she put everything in writing, so that the court was aware of the tenant that was sub leasing the house. During the preceding that they both attended because the Snake who was a subleaser did not pay the rent for months in excess of almost $7000. This was a similar pattern because of her refusal to maintain employment and rely fully on the many guys that she dealt with to pay her rent. Although at times they had similarities in their lifestyles in terms of making bad decisions and the men that they chose to deal with, one thing that Victoria always encouraged any of her associates whether male or female was to ensure that regardless of the situation that you're in make sure you position yourself to be able to take care of yourself and not be fully reliant on someone else. The point was to never give someone your everything because they decide to leave, and you ended up with nothing. Well, of course Victoria learned the lesson from the last time, so she documented the process with the rental. She felt that things were still gonna be okay and she was still gonna be authentically who she was by continuing to help people.

Victoria continued on with her life and she started to make changes that would improve her personality because there was a moment that you realize that you are surrounding yourself with people that are not at your level, then you suddenly pick up the behaviors of others including the bad language. So as Victoria started to realize that she needed to reevaluate her circle of "friends" or supposed friends. She knew that it would need to come from a bigger place in life because she never wanted to hurt people's feelings. She would only be able to make a transition that will eliminate people out of her life by means of turning to God, which in turn would prepare her to be a capable wife, in the sense that she was humble enough to know when to lead and when to follow her husband.

This was very challenging for Victoria because all of her life she had to be the leader. The followers were those that were surrounding themselves with her including her kids, so she always had to be critical of the decisions that she made. This included the people that were around her. Because the very essence of their existence, her kids depended solely on her. She did not do welfare. She did not do child support primarily because of the fact that the courts would be all involved in a situation that was not going to result in any funding which was pointless to her. She decided to just continue maintaining her livelihood by herself.

So when it came to the point where Victoria now reconnected with these friendships, her mindset had no longer been the same as it was twenty years ago and unfortunately the supposed friends ladies that she was associating with were still very much living with the idea that men needed to pay to play and that they weren't going to do anything -- they weren't going to cook or clean and be an example to the children except to show them that you needed to have a man to take care of you although you treated him like nothing and not to mention the fact that they were disrespectful to the man in every way.

A key takeaway for Victoria was when someone once called her the meanest but nicest person that they had ever met. And up until this point in her life Victoria really never cared about people's feelings especially those that were of the opposite sex. But as she grew closer to truly gaining knowledge of the Bible, she began to see the flaws that she possessed. She realized that she did have some very controlling mannerisms and that she did not always extend grace to those outside of her immediate circle, due to her own issues. She recognized that she needed to change.

You know people never think about their own actions until they start reading the Good Book. Victoria often thought about this and wanted to be the example. This meant that as she progressed in her spirituality, she needed to cut off those in her life that continued to live a life of debauchery. A part of what was necessary to learn to love what God loved and hate what God hated. Therefore, what became evident to Victoria was that not everyone was ready to accept and acknowledge the change that she was making because they never accepted who she was in the beginning. Probably because they never truly liked her and were always envious of who she was and what she had. This meant that in their mind, they always looked for an opportunity to destroy her because she thought that she was too good.

As crazy as it sounded, Victoria just could not fathom the idea that someone who literally laid in the same house that she had lived in, not once but twice, actually stabbed her in the back and went against her and talk bad about her after she was kind to them and gave them an opportunity to make substantial income… more than she had ever received in their entire life. It was unimaginable that they would do this after Victoria would provide for Snake's family when she was left desolate and without a home because of the drug dealing relationships that she engaged with. These people did not look after her but only used Victoria as a pawn in their scheme of addiction.

Yes, the actions could have been forgiven, however when acts of jealousy are done in darkness and in an attempt to destroy and assassinate Victoria's career and reputation, that was the ultimate betrayal of a friendship. The greatest outcome in this is one of humility. The fact that despite the deception, there were other snakes waiting for opportunity to then turn against Victoria because you never know who secretly hates you. But they show up when the other snakes appear.

But the greatest point of it all was the lesson of humility Victoria gained during this entire ordeal because unlike the previous situations of her past twenty years, Victoria would have behaved very differently, much like the same person that she now defended. This Snake, without any regard for anyone else but her own selfish ways now became her arch enemy because of the fact that she was attempting to now try to destroy Victoria's reputation, assassinating her character, threatening her livelihood as well as her professional brand that she built for herself. And as if that wasn't hard enough to deal with, the hard reality of it all was that after being there for decades, Victoria had to see this woman come into the place that she worked every day! To actually have to deal with her in her workplace, despite the fact that this Snake spoke badly about Victoria and told her that this time it was personal, and it was not business. To make matters worse, the Snake admitted that she could not read but then faked her whole entire professionalism because Victoria and her never discussed her knowledge or capacity, but she gave the impression that she could always do the job. In essence her manipulative tactics allowed for others to do the work for her while secretly laughing behind Victoria's back after she got her a job making more than $70,000.00 a year. What's worse is that she had previously come from a job that only paid $20.00 an hour. So, the lesson was to see how money changed this Snake although she walked around as if she didn't need any money, she was greedy for it. She learned that betrayal was a way of life and was just as dismal as the life that she lived. The trifling atmosphere that she lives in, was reflected in the same way she left the house that Victoria had rented to her in previous years.

There were days that Victoria battled within herself, and it literally took an act of God and prayer to stop her from wanting to go and beat the brakes off of this Snake because she attempted to assassinate her with lies, deceit and deception. She not only wanted the life that she saw Victoria living but actually stated to her she wanted the car that Victoria drove, and she wanted the house that Victoria purchased. And after Victoria strategically upgraded her life with her husband and her new home, this Snake also wanted to have Victoria's security because he was a man that loved and adored Victoria and that was what she wanted also. As time progressed it became even more so evident that this young lady wanted so much to be like Victoria to the extent that she changed her hair to the exact color of Victoria. Now mind you Victoria had been blonde for more than 30 years. Victoria has worn these colors consistently and this young lady never wore anything other than black in her entire life. It had become evident by the looks and the frowns and the attempts to undermine Victoria's authority when she walked in her office, that she envied her so much to the point that it had moved into an obsession.

The irony of it all is that after all she did to Victoria, she still gave her a chance because when it was time for the Snake's evaluation, Victoria knew that although she was no longer a friend to the girl, that girl still needed a means of living to take care of her children. And that was the only thing that allowed Victoria to extend to this young lady the undeserving grace that she was given.

Victoria had no understanding of how a person, given such a great opportunity to win, chose to remain in a position of a loser by refusing to educate themselves when they were hiding a very important factor which was that they could not read or write. Oftentimes this was shown in the emails that she would write in text formatting and all capital letters. It was amazing to Victoria the power of God, because after months on end and because of the structure of the organization and the timing of things, Victoria had to endure dealing with a very deceptive deceitful betrayer, that she once considered as a friend.

During this time not only did the Snake talk bad about Victoria and how Victoria was jealous about the fact that her husband had to work, but Snake's boyfriends took care of her. When that was the complete opposite of reality because the fact of the matter is that all her boyfriends can't afford to take care of her, making her fully reliant on welfare. She was also perpetrating a fraud as if she did not need anybody for anything, yet every month she received food stamps and government assistance prior to working for Victoria.

It became more and more obvious to Victoria that she was at a such a pivotal point in her life that she needed to pour into herself spiritually and yet again gain a wealth of knowledge to deal with the kind of betrayers that were puffed up with pride, having no natural affection just as the Bible foretold in the book of Timothy. As the days and weeks went on Victoria kept her distance, keeping herself busy and fully engaged personally and professionally. She was spending more time outside of the office at trainings building her professional life while creating layers of protection so that she could be protected from the Snake. At the same time, Victoria would continue to give her the same level of professionalism that she would give to everyone. However, what she understood was that this was another lesson on how to deal with uncomfortable situations and people that may not like her. This was a test for Victoria because she needed to learn how to show up at work for herself, her family, and her team that was looking at her as she was being penetrated by the negativity.

This was not only an opportunity to be strategic on how she dealt with this situation but also to be thankful for the people that she was able to extend grace to because they were also the ones that kept her abreast of situations that could potentially impact her. What situations? "You may ask. Well, it's complicated. First there was the befriending of a former colleague. They had already done the same thing to Victoria and filed a grievance against her because they lacked understanding. So, instead of accepting and acknowledging that as a person who needed help because they didn't have any understanding at the very basic level, they tried to bring someone else down as a means of deflection on the fact that they were ignorant at work and in life.

Although it was very challenging Victoria never allowed for the shots that were fired from the betrayal to penetrate so deep in her that she bled out. In fact, this helped her build up a suit of armor to protect her mentally, emotionally, spiritually, and physically. And when Victoria was ready, she forgave her. You may be wondering what you mean she forgave her; Victoria forgave the lady because that was no point in harboring resentment for a person that was never truly her friend. There was no reason to continue to harbor any ill feelings towards a person that was never on Victoria's level mentally or in any capacity. Mainly because she was not built for that. In fact, what Victoria recognized was that this person experienced trauma that never was resolved stemming from the abuse that she endured from the very men that abused her mind and body at a very young age. Because she didn't know any better the reality was that this Snake lacked self-esteem and she needed to learn how to love herself before she could ever understand what it meant to treat someone that had your back with respect.

And once Victoria forgave her, it made it easy for her to continue to acknowledge the fact that she was dead to her in her life and that she no longer needed to ever speak to her on a personal level again. All Victoria needed to do was maintain her professionalism because she still had to be a manager and manage the very person that tried to betray her. But after months of coaching and receiving spiritual encouragement and nourishment, Victoria no longer needed to get so mad that she had to turn to the behaviors of her past when she would get a "deuce deuce" and handle it with a gun. Rather she handled it with spirituality in love which is stronger than any bullet that could ever pierce someone 's heart. Victoria was able to move on to the point where the Snake did not even want to leave because she still envies Victoria but also misses her.

Unfortunately, the Snake died in a car accident with the loss of her children. And no, Victoria did not attend the funeral because they no longer had a personal connection, but she sent her condolences to the family. Tragically, this scenario had come to its end, but not without Victoria getting the victory and the reward of her new promotion to become the President of her organization.

Lessons learned – Never allow the actions of others betrayal to destroy your character as the bullet of betrayal can always be overcome by the power of self-love, consistency, faith and prayer.

ABOUT THE AUTHOR

LaKisha Love-Pettis is a native Washingtonian, wife, mother, and "Glamma", and is the published fiction author of Deuce Deuce to Love: A Shot at a Second Chance novella. She has spent over twenty years writing easy-to-understand materials for a variety of readers and is passionate about writing urban novels with digestible content that is designed to inspire and keep readers entertained. She is looking forward to the next release. LaKisha holds a degree in Business Management and Administration and is a subject matter expert in Organizational Strategic Development and Compliance.